BYZANTIUM

BYZANTIUM

Stories

BEN STROUD

Graywolf Press

This publication is made possible, in part, by the voters of Minnesota through a Minnesota State Arts Board Operating Support grant, thanks to a legislative appropriation from the arts and cultural heritage fund, and through a grant from the National Endowment for the Arts. Significant support has also been provided by Target, the McKnight Foundation, Amazon.com, and other generous contributions from foundations, corporations, and individuals. To these organizations and individuals we offer our heartfelt thanks.

Published by Graywolf Press
250 Third Avenue North, Suite 600
Minneapolis, Minnesota 55401

www.graywolfpress.org

Published in the United States of America

ISBN 978-1-55597-646-0

2 4 6 8 9 7 5 3 1
First Graywolf Printing, 2013

Library of Congress Control Number: 2013931485

Cover design: Alvaro Villanueva

Cover art: US Geological Survey Map

For Marissa

Contents

INTRODUCTION

RUMOR HAS IT THAT SHORT STORY WRITERS, nowadays, are meant to lack ambition. That short stories are best when about wee tiny things. That brief fiction should be about precious moments, only, and not about the great and grand events. That the short story's province is one of glowing epiphanies and small changes at the last minute. Short stories should not aspire to gulp down the steaming bouillabaisse of the big world; short stories should remain happy with nibbling at cute cucumber sandwiches. Who honestly believes these hollow prejudices, I do not know.

Clearly, Ben Stroud did not get this misleading e-mail, and I am so very grateful for that oversight, and I do believe the world of prose fiction is all the richer for it.

Rather than spend time trying to diagnose how the world's vision of the short story became so anemic, let us instead praise the full-blooded sweep and majesty of Stroud's imagination. Let us celebrate a writer of great bravery and artistry and deep feeling. To be sure he takes us far and wide—from Bismarck's Prussia to the conquistadors' New Spain to the Bosporus's still-Constantinople. Ben Stroud has wanderlust; this collection, *Byzantium,* is our ticket to ride.

The earliest known record we have of the black detective Jackson Hieronymus Burke—the Moor—is an advertisement he ran in several Berlin newspapers in 1873, promising discretion and modest fees. ("The Moor")

For some odd reason the concept of historical fiction has been greatly maligned among certain learned folk. To them the very phrase conjures up the lurid covers of bodice rippers set on antebellum plantations, or yet another mediocre novel about Gettysburg or the sack of Rome, or a poorly imagined biography of Caravaggio doctored up to look like fiction. It is convenient for them to forget that *War and Peace* is a historical novel, or to make bizarre rationalizations about the astonishing recent work of Hilary Mantel.

Herein rests Stroud's great courage. A story about a black sleuth in mid-nineteenth-century Berlin, "The Moor," could have been a recipe for disaster, but thanks to Stroud's Calvino-like deconstruction of narrative, a literary whirligig about mystery—masterfully done—turns the unlikely ingredients into a marvel of storytelling, unafraid of exposition, of history, of being out of fashion. It is a story that reads as if it could have been written way back then and in another language, and yet it resonates so very slyly with Obama-era preoccupations about race and origins and government and terrorism and how we try to make sense of our world.

Stroud is preternaturally wise about what it might be like to be a European man loose in the curious colonial, slave-fueled, mosquito-ridden Caribbean and the invention of a "cooling safe." The voice in "Borden's Meat Biscuit" is not show-off or drenched in dutifully researched facts, but remains convincing, a successful act of linguistic legerdemain:

> Here we paused as several negroes dressed in finery paraded before us, their masters goading them, showing them off to the city's wealthy gathered on the courthouse lawn. Timson leaned closer and whispered. "I have been in contact with agents of President Pierce. They have given me assurances."

The sentences, so often deceptively simple, tell so much with an admirable economy. Most often these stories begin in medias res. There is an implicit trust in the reader's intelligence, which makes the reading of these stories all the more engaging: it is not as much a matter of figuring things out as it is an interiority—you are experiencing this world from the inside out. Stroud respects us, expects us to be as involved, curious, and transported to these worlds as he is. We are to be flies on the wall with him.

The stories that take place in our current time have a similar fascination with travel, the wide world, the history of cities, personal histories, the mystery of history, and the history of mystery. "Amy," a story about an American in Europe and his unfaithful heart, moves us because our young man is trying to figure out his own treachery, and failing. ("I am blameless. I said: I owe no one. I said: Surely something better has been promised me.") Sad, self-deluded fellow. Just as in the story "Eraser," the protagonist grapples not just with the people around, but with what Faulkner once called "the human heart in conflict with itself."

Of course that understanding is the price of the ticket, the thing that makes Ben Stroud's stories a cut above. So we sail with him to Byzantium, to the distant shores of newly discovered countries; we witness warriors and slaves and soldiers and ship captains, but we are always reminded, taken back to the wonderful, maddening mysteries inside us all.

Yes, Ben Stroud is brave, Ben Stroud is smart, Ben Stroud is funny, Ben Stroud is a magician, Ben Stroud teaches us what it is like—past and present—to be human.

I dote on these stories, and hope you will enjoy them as much as I do.

—Randall Kenan

BYZANTIUM

BYZANTIUM

I WAS BORN a disappointment.

My father was John Lekapenos, one of the emperor Maurice's favorite generals. He had risen through the ranks from a hovel in Thessaly and had plans to establish himself—through me—among the great families. In the years he awaited my arrival, he elaborated my future career: the army, an illustrious marriage, a governorship or high ministerial position. But when I was brought to him, still smeared with my mother's blood, the first thing he saw curling toward him out of the blankets that swaddled me was the chewed red crook of my withered hand.

He must have thought it a talisman of his reverse. Not long after my birth, Maurice was overthrown and my father discharged from the army by the usurper, Phocas. He was forced to leave the camps for good, and, bloated and disheveled, he spent his days sitting in the kitchen with a pot of wine, haranguing the servants about long-ago campaigns against the Avars and the Bulgars. He talked of armies massed in the cold along the Danube, of the legion's priest bringing forth the icon of the Holy Mother, and how he would know, if the sun glinted just right against her eyes, that it would be a good day for fighting. The servants ignored him, but I always listened, snug in my hiding spot behind the oil vat, my legs folded against my chest. He loathed the sight of me, would cuff me whenever I came into his presence, but I liked to be near him, and longed to prove myself worthy of his love.

I never had the chance. He died when I was eight. He was in his bedchamber, putting on his old uniform. The Persians had been swallowing provinces whole, Phocas had in turn been deposed, and my father hoped the new emperor, Heraclius, would give him a legion. They had campaigned together years before, and he'd talked of nothing else for weeks, brightening when at last he heard the drums of Heraclius's soldiers as they entered the city. As soon as Heraclius was established in the palace and Phocas's ashes were tossed in the sea, my father prepared for court. He was to go that morning and was cleaning his sword—this he always insisted on doing himself—when he put his hand over his arm. Then he collapsed. I had hidden myself in a corner behind a chair, and when he fell I stayed there watching for nearly an hour. Eventually I crept away and left him for the servants to find.

That was the end of any hope for us. My mother kept me shut in the city house, where she looked after our dwindling fortune. I spent my days reading or hiding in the garden, listening to the servants' gossip. At my mother's insistence I always wore a specially fitted glove over my hand. I got older, grew restless. When I reached my majority a procuress was consulted and a woman brought to my chamber, and soon after that I began to sleep all day so I could prowl at night. At dusk I would escape through the back entrance to wander the dark streets, going as far as the Hippodrome. There I would watch others taking their pleasure—keeping to the shadows, my hand hidden as I studied a chariot racer leaning into a prostitute, her leg wrapped round his torso, or libertines goading a gilded crocodile in the bear pit, their bodies slurred by powders from the east. When the Persians came and encamped across the Bosporus, laying siege to the city, I went up to the roof every night to watch their attacks and then their slow retreat. When a traitor's body was dragged through the streets, I joined the mob, unnoticed, and kicked at the corpse and cursed it as the chariot pulled it toward the harbor. I had no vocation. I had no life or standing beyond our house's walls. So I lived until my twenty-eighth year, a rattling ghost in the great hive of the city.

I SAY UNTIL MY TWENTY-EIGHTH YEAR because it was in that year—the first of that brief, confident era following Heraclius's crushing victories against the Persians in the east—that an imperial courier burst into the garden where I was sitting with my mother, drinking tea, and handed me a summons. It came from the Keeper of the Seals, and when my mother saw the purple ink she began to fret. She declared I was to be given some high rank and fussed over my appearance, then decided I was to be executed and began to cry, then reversed herself a dozen times more. I didn't know what to think. The summons itself offered no hints: it only gave directions for when and how I should come to the palace. I was surprised that anyone, much less the Keeper of the Seals, would wish to seek me out. I brushed my mother away and went up to my chamber to spend the rest of the day alone.

When morning came I hired a litter to take me to the Chalke Gate, as instructed. There I showed my summons to the guards, and they admitted me to a courtyard where a large ivy grew. I knew, from one of my father's stories, what I was seeing. The ivy was nurtured from a clipping taken from the old palace at Rome, and the fountain in the courtyard's middle, surmounted by a bronze Romulus and Remus, ran with waters brought from all the empire's corners: the Tiber, the Danube, a spring in Syria, the upper reaches of the Nile. Just beyond the fountain, three men were contesting with an elephant, a spoil from the wars. A crowd of servants and soldiers had gathered to watch them fit gold covers onto his tusks. Some had their arms to their noses in imitation of the elephant's trunk, and were whistling, trying to get him to trumpet.

Stacks of crates filled the other side of the courtyard, and it was from behind one of these that a eunuch, spare and with a shaved head, emerged. Squeezing out of his hiding place, he dusted himself off and came up to me and demanded the summons. After he read it he gave me an oddly close look. Then he ordered me out of the litter and took me past the elephant and through a guarded archway. We walked a few steps down a grand corridor of white marble before he stopped and pulled back a tapestry. Behind it, a narrow passageway snaked off into darkness. He went in ahead of me, guiding me by the sleeve, running his other hand along the brick and repeating something to himself. When we came to a tiny iron door he stopped and faced me.

"Say nothing," he said. "Stand and wait." Then, twisting and pulling a ring in the door, he opened it and told me to step through.

I had to stoop to clear the topstone, and by the time I stood on the other side, the door had shut behind me. Turning back, I could barely make it out, its lines fitting smoothly into the wall. But as I looked around me I soon forgot the door. The room glittered with gold. A stream ran through its middle, bounded by golden shrubs hung with carnelian fruits and silver briars hooked with thorns. High green trees of mosaic climbed the walls to the ceiling, where light fell from shafts and a sun glided on a circuit. In the center of the ceiling's vault, God stared down, His hair flowing, His eyes gleaming in angry judgment. I knew where I was. I had always thought the Chamber of the Golden Meadow a legend, like the chamber that contained a living map of the sea. I looked again at the silver briars. I had heard it said that some of the thorns were poisoned; only the emperor knew which ones. He would meet his spies and servants here and take them for a stroll alongside the briars. If he grew displeased, he would give his interlocutor a nudge, and the unfortunate's soul would be parted from his body by morning.

The stream trickled, the sun clicked on its track, and I waited, even more uncertain of what was to come.

A half hour passed, then another. Finally, a door on the far side of the room opened. It wasn't the Keeper of the Seals who stepped through but Heraclius himself. The door closed behind him and he took a few steps toward me, then stopped. He was dressed in a simple tunic and a studded leather belt. His beard, grayed by his campaigns, hung below his chest. I stood still as stone—to suddenly be alone with the emperor, the man on whom all the eyes of the known world were fixed!—before it dawned on me that I was to go to him. I did so, bowing two or three times (in my nervousness I forgot the specific demands of protocol), and once I came near he put his hand on my shoulder and looked me over with his fading blue eyes.

"You are Eusebios Lekapenos, John Lekapenos's son?"

"I am," I answered, keeping my head bowed.

"Show me your hand."

He did not specify, but it was not difficult to guess which he meant. I brought my withered hand forward, slipped off the glove, and let him see. He glanced at the bent knobs that were my fingers, the wrinkled crook that was my wrist, then motioned for me to put the glove back on. Once I'd done this, he took me by the arm and led me toward the stream.

"I knew your father," he said. "We campaigned together. It was a shame that—" He broke off, then nodded at me. After a moment's silence, he started again, using a tone that, coupled with the unsubtle shift in subject, told me he was getting down to business. With a shiver I realized he was guiding me along the silver briars. "I recall hearing a story that when you were a child you visited several holy men, each of whom promised to heal your hand for you."

The story was true. Two years after my father died, my mother conceived the notion that a holy man could heal my hand, and she broke our isolation to take me through the streets to find one. In those days, as now, holy men flocked to the capital. They set themselves up in the houses of the rich, where they dressed in rags, refused baths, and spat out the delicate morsels offered them at dinner while shouting about fleshpots and the temptations of Babylon. Others, claiming to shun the world, lived in caves or on mountaintops a day's walk from the city, where they received crowds. And yet others set themselves on pillars in the streets and in the fora, shaking their beards at the people below and warning of coming cataclysms. The first holy man she took me to, chubby and with matted hair, grabbed my hand, put it to his mouth, and licked it. The second made me wait in his cave for two hours while he received other pilgrims, then told me that my hand was twisted because the devil had taken hold of it and that I must repent of my sins. The third spat at me from his pillar, claiming that would be enough, and the fourth told me to fast for six days and then return, by which time, forgetting me, he had left the city. Only with the fifth did I rebel. He had set himself up in one of the grandest houses on the Golden Horn, and promised to heal my hand if I would show my faith in his works by plunging it into a pot of boiling water. I had been given hope, I had believed in them, and when the healings failed I had blamed myself. But as I trembled beneath this holy man's half-blind stare, his toothless scowl, I understood: he was a charlatan. They were all charlatans. I kicked the pot over, scalding the holy man's legs, and ran out. The story passed through the city for a week—this I heard from the servants—before dying out. It was painful to recall, and I wondered why the emperor was interested.

"I visited five," I said.

"And they could do nothing for you," he said, "except mock your misfortune."

I didn't know what answer to give, so I remained silent. We reached the end of the stream.

"Have you heard the stories about the monk Theodosios?"

I nodded. Everyone had.

"Let me tell you another," the emperor said as we crossed a footbridge and started walking up the other side. "The emperor Maurice had a son named Theodosios. He was slaughtered by Phocas alongside his father, but because his head was not sent back to the city, some claim he escaped and fled to the Persians for safety." The emperor paused for a moment. He glanced up at the ceiling, to the eyes of God. Then he continued. "That story belongs to the past, and yet only a week ago one of my spies brought me a troubling report. In both Aleppo and Antioch he heard a rumor that Maurice's Theodosios and this monk are the same, and that this monk has a claim to the throne as the rightful heir."

The emperor squeezed my arm, nudged me ever so slightly toward the briars.

"It is a foolish rumor, and yet it disturbs my sleep."

"But, Emperor, surely no one would—"

At a look from Heraclius I quieted. He was at the height of his glory. He had crushed the Persian king Chosroes, regained the eastern provinces, restored the True Cross to Jerusalem, and ordered the golden saddle of the general Shahrbaraz beaten into coins for the poor. It was said that he had saved the empire, and now it would last a thousand more years. Meanwhile, Theodosios was the object of vague stories that had only recently spread to the city. He was a monk at the Monastery of the Five Holy Martyrs, in the desert between Jerusalem and the Dead Sea, and was said to be a master ascetic and to have seen visions of the Holy Mother denouncing the Monophysites. He never stirred from his monastery, and as yet only a few pilgrims from Constantinople had reported seeing him—and they never spoke of the encounter except in the most general terms. The bronze likenesses of his head that merchants sold in the Mese were each unlike the other, because no one knew what he looked like, and his fame paled when compared to that of Father Eustachios, who lived at Mount Athos and allegedly spoke with the angels, or that of Severus, an Egyptian who was walking on his knees from Alexandria to our city and stopping only to deliver homilies.

What, I thought, could Heraclius fear from such a man? But then one need only consider his three predecessors, whose fates I'd studied as a child: Tiberius Constantine poisoned, Maurice made to watch the slaughter of his family before being slaughtered himself, and Phocas hanged then burned in the Bronze Bull. It seemed Heraclius had learned that most vital lesson of ruling: for an emperor, natural death is rare. All it takes is for the people to be disappointed—for the corn boats from Alexandria to sink, for the Avars to make unexpected advances on the frontier—and with a single riot, the Christ-Faithful emperor, Autocrat of all the

Romans, can fall. The people only need a candidate to replace him, a candidate much like this monk Theodosios.

"You have led an aimless life," the emperor said once he saw I understood. "A life without meaning, unworthy of your father. I offer you a chance to honor him and to serve the empire. I have need of a man with no fear of holy men, a man not known as one of my spies or assassins, a man who yearns for the glory of which he has been deprived." I felt his fingers clench my arm. "I believe I have found this man," he said.

His words sank like a stone weight. But there was no time for consideration. "You have, Emperor," I said.

At that he guided me from the thorns. "I will not forget your service," he said, then touched one of the carnelian berries. The door in the wall opened.

The eunuch was waiting for me. He rushed me back through the narrow passage and whispered hurriedly in my ear. "Do not kill him," he said. "The emperor is superstitious and will not allow the death of a monk. You are to geld him, for a eunuch can never hope to be emperor." He flashed me a grim smile, then handed me a knife and a leather purse filled with coins. "You will bring back the fruits of your gelding in the purse. For this the emperor will reward you with rank and gold." We reached the courtyard just as he finished. Once there, he gave me a shove toward the waiting litter, then disappeared behind the crates. One of the slaves was holding open the litter's curtain; I signed for him to wait. The elephant I had seen when I arrived was now enraged. A gold cover had been set on one of his tusks, but the elephant had crushed the other cover with his foot and, to the delight of the crowd, was now rising on his hind legs and trumpeting as his caretakers scrambled to tame him. It was a rare spectacle, and even in my state I thought it worth a moment's pause.

WHEN I TOLD MY MOTHER the emperor had trusted me with a commission, she fell to her knees and kissed my hem, swearing she would pray each day in the Church of the Holy Wisdom for my success. I fled to my chamber and prepared to leave. I saw no reason to wait. Rather, I was eager to have the thing done. Rattled from my meeting with Heraclius, I seemed unable to loose the tangle of thoughts that had taken possession of me since our stroll in the Golden Meadow. There was insult: this was an executioner's task, the kind you hire a wretch from the streets to accomplish. And there was fear: where would I begin, how would I bring myself to castrate a man? But twisted among these, growing like a summer vine, was pride. At last I could do something worthy, at last I could, in my way, serve the empire like my father. I sailed that very night, using the emperor's gold to buy passage on a Cretan trader, and all during the voyage I stayed in my cabin and practiced. I wrestled with a sack of grain, cut at slabs of meat with the knife. As the ship rocked and the sack lurched, I trained myself to pin it with my lame hand.

My regimen was not perfect, but by the time I landed at Caesarea I felt I had become, if not expert, adequate to the emperor's task. I purchased three donkeys and spent the day loading them with provisions, then joined a caravan for Jerusalem. Once we reached the city, still in ruins from the Persian occupation, I stopped only to take a meal. Let it be finished, I thought, and that night I hired a guide and set out for the desert.

I ARRIVED AT THE Monastery of the Five Holy Martyrs at noon the next day. The monastery, a collection of paths and caves and small stone buildings, lay scattered along the side of a dry ravine, and as soon as I rounded the last bend, a monk came running down from its tower. He intercepted me and introduced himself as Brother Sergios. He was young, just out of boyhood—his blond eyes and smooth skin would have caused a stir in the baths—and it was his task, he told me, to aid visitors.

"Where do you come from?" he asked, turning around and walking backward to face me. He had taken the donkeys in hand and was leading me toward the guesthouse, which stood, beneath the rest of the monastery, on a ledge overlooking the ravine's dry bottom.

"Constantinople," I answered.

"The capital," he said, releasing the two words with a wondered hush. "We don't get many visitors from the capital. The higoumen says it is a pit of devils."

"That may well be so," I said. Brother Sergios laughed, then tied up the donkeys and showed me into the guesthouse. I had to stifle my revulsion. The guesthouse was a long, low edifice of stone and mud. In its one large room men slept like hogs, one against the other, while others talked as they ate a sorrowful-looking gruel and played a game with stone pegs. Brother Sergios told me they were a party of farmers, come to pray for their crops, and that the others included a rug merchant and his daughter from Jericho—come to be near Theodosios—and two water sellers from Bethel, who were waiting for one of the monks, a Brother Alexander, to settle a dispute between them.

"There are no other quarters?" I asked.

"No," Brother Sergios said. "Here everyone shares equally."

Fortunately, I had considered this. On the ship I had decided my plan. I had briefly thought of arriving as a humble suppliant, but felt an aversion to trading on my hand and didn't want to risk the monks presenting me to someone besides Theodosios. Instead, I would arrive as a great personage from court, impressing the rustics to the point that they dared not refuse my requests. I had bought accordingly in Caesarea. The far back corner of the guesthouse was empty and I claimed it. While Brother Sergios swept away the dust, I enlisted two of the farmers to unload the donkeys. On my orders, they cut open the bundles and pulled out carpets and pillows and the unassembled pieces of a chair with ivory facings. I had them hang several of the carpets from the ceiling to form walls and spread another on the floor, along with the cushions, and then fit the chair together and set it in the carpet's middle. I now had a private bedchamber and receiving room as luxurious as one could hope. I sent the two farmers back to the common room but kept Brother Sergios near me.

"You must be hungry," he said, and indicated a tall earthen pot from which I'd seen some of the others taking their gruel.

"Not for that," I said, then pulled the carpets to and went to my chair, where I struck my best imperial pose. It took all my concentration to maintain the act: the whole time, even as I unwrapped a smoked duck stuffed with larks and berries, I kept my withered hand in my tunic. "I shall meet with Theodosios at his convenience," I said.

Brother Sergios shook his head. "Brother Theodosios has taken a vow of solitude," he said. "He meets with no one, unless they are possessed by demons. I believe I'd be correct in guessing you are not so afflicted?"

"I am not," I said, and slipped a piece of the dark duck meat into my mouth.

"Just last week he drove off a demon who had been tempting a brother monk into acedia, and not two weeks before—"

"Tell him I come from the emperor," I said.

Brother Sergios blushed, as if I'd somehow blundered. "Oh, I am not allowed to speak to him," he said. "But I will inform the higoumen."

Brother Sergios left me then, and I continued picking at the duck as I stared out the slit of a window that was my chamber's sole source of light. It faced onto the monastery above, which I now saw was a labyrinth. I had not considered this while preparing myself on the boat, and for a moment I despaired. How would I find, among that maze of paths, that tangle of caves and cells, the man I sought, if no one would take me to him?

I SET THIS QUANDARY ASIDE—surely, in time, the monastery would unlock itself to me—and decided to make myself more comfortable. I found I had adjusted rather well to my role as the man from Constantinople, and, as my provisions would not last, I hired a goatherd to cook for me. That first night he roasted a kid on a spit. Thinking it wise to win over the other lodgers, once I'd eaten my fill I offered the rest of the carcass to them. They rushed forward, all gentleness forgotten as they shoved each other and thrust their grubby fingers at the meat.

After they each had taken a portion, the lodgers fell to laughing and boasting. I retired to my corner to read by my lamp. I was only two lines into the scroll (a farce featuring two Armenian princes) when I heard the rest of the guesthouse suddenly fall silent. My interest piqued, I listened closely, and after several seconds I heard the silence break into mumbled prayers. I stood up and went to the edge of my curtain to see what had happened. A stooped old man, leaning on a cane, his beard nearly sweeping the floor, had entered the room. He was making the sign of the cross over the other lodgers, and when he finished, he started toward me with a slow, crooked walk. I left the curtain and returned to my chair. I tried to keep reading, but the words slipped past my mind. All I could hear were the steady, solemn footsteps of the old man.

He entered my quarters, his footsteps muffling as he crossed onto the carpet. I continued my pretense of reading, but that didn't seem to bother him.

"My name is Andrew," he said in a voice more commanding than what I'd expected from one so frail. "I am the higoumen of this monastery."

At that I looked up. "I am honored by your presence," I said. "Would you care to sit?"

"On one of your silk cushions, such cushions as line the halls of Hell, corrupting the body with false comfort?" he answered, spitting as he spoke, his face turning an apoplectic hue. "Bah! Brother Sergios has told me of you. He said a great man had come from Constantinople, to which I now say, by what measure of greatness? These carpets, that chair? All such stuff that passes from this earth? They might affect young Brother Sergios, but not me. Better for you to have brought nothing and cleaved to humility."

"If these cushions and carpets offend you, higoumen—" I began, but he cut me off.

"Offend me? I do not notice them. I only warn you for your soul. But enough. Tell me why you have come, worldling."

"Very well," I said. "I come at Heraclius's behest. He has heard the stories of Theodosios and has asked me to meet with him in private and investigate their truth."

This last, of course, was my own invention.

"Bah," the higoumen replied, waving his hand at me as if to send me away. "Let the emperor have more faith. Brother Theodosios does not seek fame, nor does he indulge in vanity. He has hidden himself in the mountain so that he may continue his struggle unbothered. Pack up and return to your pit of sin."

"Father Andrew," I said, "I will remain here until I see Theodosios."

"In that case, as you will have much time to yourself, I suggest you take up prayer."

At that he turned and hobbled as fast as he could out of my chamber. There erupted another mumbling of prayers when he reached the common room. Then he left, and I heard a crush and scuffle. I went to the parting in my carpets to look: the lodgers, in rushing toward the kid once more, had toppled the spit.

THE NEXT DAYS PASSED IN FRUSTRATION. The monks could not force me to leave—they were pledged to hospitality—but neither would they let me see Theodosios. So I tried on my own. Twice I crept up the ravine's side at night to search for his cave, stumbling and slipping as I climbed blindly in the dark. Both times I was quickly found and escorted back to the guesthouse. Once I offered three gold solidi to a monk who'd come down to pray with the farmers about their crops. He said nothing, only crossed himself and backed away, as if he'd just had a brush with Satan. Even when I asked about Theodosios—it troubled me that I knew so little about him—the monks shook their heads and shied from me. I only stopped when Brother Sergios explained that Theodosios, in his humility, had asked the other monks to speak of him as little as possible. Five days in, I was certain I had my break. A man arrived complaining of a demon in his tongue. He would be taken to Theodosios, and I need only wait and watch. I spent all day in my quarters, next to the window, pretending to write letters by its light. But the monks came for the man at night, before the moon had risen, and I could see nothing of where they took him.

My efforts were clumsy, and by the end of the week I'd gained nothing. But I learned something in growing up as I had, in longing to be near a father who couldn't stand the sight of me: I learned to notice.

I was bored. My only distraction was to walk up and down the ravine or gamble with one of the lodgers who'd brought dice. Even in the years of my greatest isolation I had been able to talk to the servants, watch the city from the roof, and, when the need took me, drift through the night crowds. A week after I arrived at the monastery, I sent to Jerusalem for an actress. She came the next evening and set up outside the guesthouse. I brought my chair out to sit before her, and the other lodgers came out and reclined along the ledge. We watched as she performed the Rape of Lucretia—she played well the shocked virgin, her hand cupping her mouth—then Leda and the Swan. It was during this last, done with an ingeniously stuffed bird and a skillful gyration of her hips, that I noticed Brother Sergios. Since my attempted wanderings into the monastery, he had been ordered to stay outside the guesthouse. Normally he spent his hours in prayer, eyes hooded as he mumbled and rocked. But when I glanced his way, I saw he'd ceased praying and was watching the actress, who at that moment let fly another startled shout of pleasure.

The next day I sent for a flutist and a dancer, and after that, tumblers. I monitored Brother Sergios. Each night he struggled with his prayers, opening one eye, then the other, before giving in to the spectacle. He applauded the flutist and his dancer, gasped at the tumblers' tricks. The evening after the tumblers, he asked me about Constantinople, and I told him about the races in the Hippodrome and the painted women in the market, about the ships in the harbor from every sea and the warrens of winding streets that seemed to lead to the ends of the earth. The next night I hired another actress, who presented scenes from the life of the empress Theodora, then a conjurer who made cups disappear and told fortunes by burning a plucked hair. Brother Sergios had rushed forward, offering one of his own.

It was the clown who came on the sixth evening that proved to be my masterstroke. He juggled firebrands while repeating rhymes about female genitalia. Brother Sergios's laughter echoed up and down the ravine. It must have caught the ears of the higoumen, for the next morning, as I was sitting in my corner of the guesthouse during the hot midday hours, reading, I heard again a hush among the other lodgers and the thump of a walking stick on the stone floor.

"Corrupter!" the higoumen shouted as soon as he passed through the hanging carpets. "Violator! Give up your tricks and leave us!"

"I prefer to stay," I said.

"You are a devil," he said. "I shall cast you out."

"I am a guest, and you are sworn to hospitality. Or have you already forgotten the lesson in the Miracle of the Cisterns, Most Holy Father?" In the Miracle of the Cisterns, one of the more widely repeated wonders of Theodosios, the monks had been punished for putting their own needs above those of their guests.

At my mention of the miracle, the higoumen's face reddened. He raised his stick and held it before him as if he were going to strike me, but a moment later he put it down and burst out with a chain of prayers. Then he turned and left without a further word.

That afternoon, Brother Sergios visited me. He bowed and reported that Theodosios had agreed to receive me, and that he,

Brother Sergios, would take me to him at nightfall. I sent away the magician who had just arrived and for the rest of the day hid in my quarters.

I HAD PRACTICED ON THE SHIP, and thoughts of the gelding had weighed ever in the back of my mind, but only now was I confronted with the imminence of my task. Very soon, I would have to cut the flesh of another man, a man I'd not yet even seen. When my father was my age, he led a sortie across the Danube and captured an Avar prince. I wondered what he had thought in the hours before setting out. I tried to prepare myself, to ready my mind, to imagine the emperor's wrath, the silver thorns in the Chamber of the Golden Meadow that awaited me if I failed. But nothing worked. I could only wait and hope I acted well when the moment came.

Brother Sergios entered my quarters in the first minutes of dusk. All day he had been absent from his watching post—attending, I imagined, to the offices of repentance. He refused to meet my eye, and as he led me up the ravine's side he kept his silence, so I kept mine. I felt for him, but I had my own concerns.

The moon was still down, but the last streak of red remained glowing in the west. We soon passed into a part of the monastery that Brother Sergios was unfamiliar with. At each fork in the trail he had to stop and consult his memory before choosing the way. Pitch-dark caves echoed with the mumble of prayers, and desert creatures, invisible in the blackness, skittered from our path. After a stiff climb we suddenly topped the ravine, the night sky leaping into place all around us. We only stayed a moment, long enough for Brother Sergios to find a new path, marked by a small stack of pebbles, and lead me back down. A few yards in, we crossed a fissure in the rock by a bridge of dried sticks. The bridge squeaked and shifted beneath our weight, and once we were over, Brother Sergios halted and pointed to a far boulder. Its surface flickered with reflected lamplight, the source deep in an unseen hollow. We had arrived.

I stood for a moment, paralyzed. I was here at last, and had to master several flutters of panic. When I finally turned to Brother Sergios, to ask if it was time, I saw he had gone.

"Come," a voice said, from the same direction as the light. I stepped forward, toward the boulder and into the hollow, which opened into the wide mouth of a grotto. Inside, a monk my age stood with his hands clasped before him. Beside him sat a man weaving a basket, his body made of lumps, his jaw too large for his face. Next to this man was the lamp, and before him lay a reed mat.

"The mat is for you," the monk said.

I couldn't understand. What game was Theodosios playing, having me sit before this unfortunate while he watched? Just as I wondered this, the unfortunate moaned, like a man with an over-thick tongue, and the monk said to me, "I ask your indulgence. I wish to finish the basket. Two of the brothers are taking another load to Jerusalem tomorrow."

It took a moment, but, with a prickle of surprise somewhere beneath my gut, I understood. The monstrous imbecile was Theodosios. The other monk was translating for him. Briefly, the thought crossed my mind: was my task necessary? But Heraclius had given his command. Besides, they'd made emperors from worse. I sat and watched as Theodosios wove the basket's rim, twisting and tucking the reed at an expert pace.

He finished the basket, set it aside, then began to moan at me. "I apologize," the monk translated. "I should have received you the moment you came. It was vanity that made me think I could hide myself from the world while others cannot. For this vanity, for this pride, I allowed one of our brothers, whose soul should be my greatest care, to be corrupted."

Theodosios looked at me. I wasn't sure what he wanted, so I said, "For my part, I forgive you."

This seemed to offer him some solace. He smiled crookedly

and nodded. He was about to speak again when he stopped and fixed me with a stare. His left eye was not level in his head—it was as if it had been pushed into the raw dough of his face—and it was with this eye that he studied me. He let out a low moan. "Something troubles you," the monk translated. "Speak." "There's nothing," I said. Another low moan. "I know what it is," the monk translated. "I can see it in you."

"I tell you there's nothing," I said, but I rose. I had sent a message to my goatherd to have a horse waiting up the ravine. I could be in the crowds of Jerusalem, disappeared, by noon.

Before I could take a step, Theodosios leaned forward and grabbed my ankle and held me fast. He uttered a long chain of hurried moans. "I see your father in the garden. He's throwing his glass. I see you hiding and weeping and pitying yourself. I see the black knot within you. It was not tied by the devil and it was not tied by God—"

I twisted free. "That is not why I came," I said, struggling to keep my voice from shaking.

Theodosios let out another string of moans. "You may hold on to your pains if you wish," the monk translated. "I have been told your mission. They speak of me in the imperial court and have asked you to investigate my works."

I said nothing, only waited.

"Listen," the monk translated. "I have a message for you to take back. The people and the priests devote themselves to quibbles. They are old women arguing in the market as a flood rises to overtake the city. The emperor is a blind beast, thinking every trembling leaf the tread of a hunter, and he feels not the world shifting beneath him. We are at the gate of perdition. Our sins will be judged, and in these times we must all be brother to one another."

"Proof," I interrupted. "I have come for proof."

And for a moment I believed this was my true mission. Theodosios remained quiet for some time. Then he closed his eyes and mumbled something the monk did not translate. When he finished, the monk—I never learned his name—went to the back of the grotto and fetched a small jar.

"Give me your broken hand," the monk translated as Theodosios held out his own hand, palm open.

I hesitated. I had not expected this.

"Give me your hand," the monk repeated.

I had no choice. I pulled my hand from my tunic and put it in Theodosios's. With a solemn nod he sent the translator away, then peeled off the glove and poured ointment from the jar and began rubbing it into my skin. For ten minutes, he kissed the crook of my wrist, the knobs of my fingers. He scrubbed my hand with his hair, and the whole time moaned prayers. I watched his face and I watched my hand. When he ceased his efforts it remained as withered as ever.

Theodosios studied my hand, his already misshapen face contorted in bafflement. He looked up to the grotto's ceiling, moaned something, then rubbed more ointment into my fingers and wrist. He signed for me to wait and tried to communicate, with moans and shaking head, that he didn't understand. But I did. I saw again the holy men who had humiliated me in my youth: their hollow smiles, their empty promises, their mocking eyes. Here was another with his finely honed act, playing me for a fool. It seemed Heraclius knew well what he was doing when he chose me. I burned with shame—for a moment Theodosios had gotten to me—and I felt no hesitation now.

Before he could take my hand again, I leapt onto Theodosios and pinned him with my knees. He moaned; I covered his mouth with my good hand. He struggled, pulling himself up; I shoved him back to the grotto's floor. With a jerk, I forced up his habit, then felt in my tunic for the knife, squeezing its handle between my stunted fingers. He was screaming and struggling. I had no time. Taking my other hand from his mouth, I gave him a cuff to quiet him and grabbed his testicles, lifting them from his body, and made the cut. With a single tug the knife sliced cleanly through the boneless flesh and it was done. Theodosios twisted beneath me, his bellowing mouth bent in a terrible grimace, but I felt a quiver of calm relief. It hadn't been nearly as hard as I'd feared.

The other monk had reappeared in the grotto's entrance, panting and silent, in shock, and I was recalled to my senses. I stuffed Theodosios's testicles in the leather purse and pushed my way out. Once across the footbridge, I fled blindly, but fleeing was easy. The monastery was only a labyrinth when you were looking for someone, not when you were running away. I slipped and slid on the paths, shoved my way through the monks who'd come from their caves at the sound of Theodosios's howls. By the time I made it to the bottom of the ravine, they were sounding the monastery's wooden bell. Its furious *tock* filled the valley. I skirted the guesthouse—the lodgers had emptied out onto the ledge—and ran to where the goatherd was waiting with the horse.

"Sir," he said as he helped me up. "What's happened, why are they ringing the bell?"

"Don't worry yourself about that," I said.

He was still holding the reins when he pulled back and pointed. "Sir," he said. "Your hand."

I looked down. It was ribboned with blood. I gave the goatherd a kick, took the reins, and spurred the horse. But I soon lost track of where I was going. Too startled to think, I kept looking in disbelief at my hand. The goatherd had not seen what I had seen. He had seen only the blood. I saw something more. Where the blood had run over my hand, it had made the withered flesh whole.

I PASSED THE NEXT DAY in a wandering stupor. I am still uncertain how I made it out of the desert. As I sat upon my horse, a lightness coursed through my veins. My mind reeled: each explanation I could fathom crumbled in the face of another. He knew what I'd come to do; he didn't know. He was a true holy man; it was some sort of new charlatan's trick. The hand was a blessing from God; it was a curse of the devil. I felt a sickness for what I had done, but then I would look at my hand. I had washed it and wiped it clean, and as my horse ambled and nibbled at dry grass, I gazed at its new perfection. I flexed its fingers, traced the straightened, flat pan of its palm. I held both hands side by side. They were mirrors of each other, though the healed hand was smoother, pinker.

Just before sunset, I reached the orchards outside Jerusalem. I rode around the city, headed straight to the coast as I imagined the new life that awaited me: a place in court, prominent seats in the Hippodrome, our family restored to its rightful place. Perhaps it wouldn't be too late for me to take a command, some squadron on the Dalmatian frontier. If any asked about my hand, I would say I had visited a sulfur spring in Greece and was treated by a physician. But surely few would ask. I was unknown. Only the emperor's long-memoried informants had any idea who I was. That, I decided, would soon be changed.

BY THE TIME I RETURNED TO CONSTANTINOPLE, I had regained enough of my reason to be fearful. I didn't know what news had reached the city, or what the reaction might be: perhaps mobs filled the fora, clamoring for my death. Once off the boat, I hid in the crowds and gleaned the conversations of passersby. I trailed parties of beggars through the markets, sat with the mad outside church doors. Only among these did I feel safe, unseen. Within hours of my arrival, while huddling outside the Church of the Holy Wisdom with a pair of moaners, I heard the first rumors of the gelding. Some passing monks were discussing it, and I was relieved: they had the story wrong. "The assassin was a Monophysite," one declared, setting the others off. "No, I heard he was a Jew." "No, a devil." "It was a punishment, for pride." The monks all frowned, though on one I detected a stifled smile. By evening, a troupe of clowns had spread through the city, portraying the surprised Theodosios and his veiled attacker.

After another day of listening, satisfied I wasn't hunted, I made my way to the Chalke Gate, where I whispered my presence to one of the guards. I was expected. Within a minute, the eunuch from before came and showed me directly to the Chamber of the Golden Meadow. There I knelt and waited, nervous, every organ beneath my chest grown cold, my palms and my scalp beading with sweat. I returned triumphant, but what if Heraclius had lied to me? What if my reward awaited me here, among the silver thorns? I glanced at them now, wishing I knew which were poison-tipped.

I had just begun counting the drops of sweat falling from my forehead when the emperor burst through the door and strode toward me, roaring gleefully. "I have heard the reports!" he said. "There'll be no more talk of a monk on the throne, that's for certain."

I kept my head bowed. Warm relief flooded through me. My fears now seemed groundless.

"Your father would be pleased," Heraclius went on as he stood over me. "You have done your duty." Then he chuckled and seemed to play out the gelding in his mind, for I saw him make a flick of the wrist like a man slicing grapes from a vine. After two more of these flicks, he asked, "Do you have them?"

I bowed lower and offered up the leather purse, which I had kept tied to my tunic since fleeing the monastery. Before leading me to the Chamber, the eunuch had made sure I remembered to bring Theodosios's testicles. It seemed Heraclius possessed a cabinet near his bed in which he stored, preserved in vinegar, similar artifacts taken from vanquished pretenders and Persian generals.

"Tell me," the emperor said when he finished prodding the purse, "did he squeal?"

"He screamed in pain, Emperor," I answered, speaking as evenly as I could.

"Very good," the emperor said, then, after losing himself in throught and chuckling once more, "you may go."

I hesitated. I felt as if I couldn't move and before I knew what I was doing I called out, "Emperor." He looked back—he had already stepped toward his door—and I held up my bared hand. The stream purled beneath the silver briars. Above us the eyes of God stared, fixed in stone and gilded glass.

"Theodosios?" Heraclius asked, his face gone pale.

I nodded.

The emperor came to where I was kneeling. He grabbed me by the wrist and examined my hand. "So he was genuine," he said. "That is unfortunate."

I quaked. On the ship back, as my fascination with my hand settled into calm acceptance, doubts began to plague me. Surely I had committed a grievous crime. Now I was certain I would be tipped into the briars.

"I will tell you something," the emperor said. "It is by far not the worst thing I have had done." He pulled me close. I could see a narrowness in his gaze, the tired narrowness of one long hunted, of a bear in its final moments in the pit as the dogs close in. I thought of Theodosios's vision, of the emperor as a frightened, blind beast, and waited for the shove, for the prick of the thorns. But before I could close my eyes the emperor let me go, pressed the carnelian berry, and sent me away.

RELEASED FROM THE CHALKE GATE, I picked my way through the Mese's undulant, squabbling crowd of merchants. Dazed still from my meeting with Heraclius, I paid no attention to the clothier who thrust a wool mantle into my hands, to the tin seller who danced before me, his cups dangling from his arms. I was headed, at last, for home.

"Eusebios," my mother said when I stepped into the courtyard. She stood there as if knocked still, whispered a veneration to the

Holy Mother, then clutched me and wept into my shoulder. My heart—this surprised me—swelled, and for a moment I forgot all that I had done. Only when she pulled away did she see my hand. "How?" she asked, seizing it and pulling it close to her eyes. I started on about a Grecian spring, but she scoffed. So I told her the truth, and in the telling I felt suddenly proud. What I had done was difficult. I had served the emperor. And mightn't the hand be a sign that I had done right? But before I could finish, my mother let me go and backed away.

"That was you?" she said. Her flesh seemed to have turned ashen. "You have mocked God," she pronounced. "That hand is a curse. He has shown you His power." She looked at me, her face stricken with disappointment, then fled from the courtyard to her room, where she shut herself for the rest of the afternoon.

For several days after, she avoided me. Then one morning, a servant came to my bedchamber as I was dressing and presented me with a new glove. I didn't need to ask who had sent it. I wanted to throw it across the room. I wanted to send it back torn. But I put it on. When I went down, my mother was waiting in the courtyard. With a brief flick of her eyes she confirmed the glove's presence. After that, she never again mentioned my hand.

I WAS NOW A GREAT MAN. I rode through the city, shouting across the rabble to other young courtiers I had met, and involved myself in Hippodrome politics, supporting the Blues, as my father had, and standing feasts for the chariot racers. Heraclius had kept his promise of reward. It had been announced that at the Feast of Palms I would be granted an income and subpatrician rank, which, among other privileges, would allow me a title, the use of blue ink, and the right to be drawn in a carriage by four brown ponies.

A month after my return, I received perhaps my greatest honor: an invitation to dine at an imperial banquet in the Triclinium of the Nineteen Couches. I sent for the tailor and commissioned a new tunic, and when the evening came I daubed myself with scent. As I was leaving, I could hear my mother in her room, murmuring her constant prayers. I ignored them, and once I stepped into my litter I slipped off my glove and tossed it to a servant. At the dinner I was given a poor seat, far from Heraclius—a hundred men separated us—and near the twelve paupers. But I was there. I belonged. The musicians played airy tunes, the tableware glittered in the lamplight, and the emperor, I was certain, had looked at me with approval.

It was when the wine was being poured and I had begun talking to the youth on my right—the son of a Bithynian tax farmer—that one of the paupers, seated toward the middle of their table, leapt up and hissed at me. I had noticed him giving me twitchy glances and had hoped it would end there. His beard was matted, his skin burnt to leather, and after he hissed again he pointed at me with a pheasant bone and shouted, "Blood on his hand!" The entire room fell silent and stared. I sat as still as I could, and as my heart beat I felt each pulse's tremble. Someone seemed to be squeezing my chest, denying me all but the tiniest spoonfuls of breath. The rumors of Theodosios's gelding had grown more detailed in the recent days, and I feared that at last I had been caught out.

But then a soldier pulled the pauper from where he stood. The next dish, turtles cooked in their shells, was brought. Everyone returned to their conversations as if nothing had happened. They were all well-practiced courtiers. A madman, two or three said. The Bithynian began rattling on about some gossip he'd heard concerning the Greens' new bearkeeper, and at the next table a general from the east assured his neighbors that the recent Saracen unrest, during which they'd proclaimed a prophet (such an idea raised laughter), would be put down by winter. And yet I couldn't return so easily. Those latest rumors held that Theodosios had retreated farther into the desert, and since that night there had been no new miracles. As I reclined, I saw again his twisted face. I heard his cries, felt his bloody manhood in my palm, and thought of what my mother had said. A curse.

The musicians changed songs. A slave reached over my shoulder and pulled apart my turtle shell. I hid my hand under the table and forced my mouth into a smile. I had served an empire that would last forever, I had become the son my father died wanting. There could be no regret.

EAST TEXAS LUMBER

BACK FROM LUNCH, I stood in the early June sun pulling two-by-sixes for somebody else's load when Mike, the yard manager, came out of the office and yelled, "All right, Brian, I've got an easy one for you and Jimmy."

It took me half a moment to register what he was saying. My mind had nestled itself against the secret, moon-pale skin between the buttons of this shirt Angela sometimes wore at The Hangout, the church club over in the strip mall where the Safeway used to be. But as soon as I did I dropped the two-by-six midpull and said to Mike, "Let me kneel down before you. I swear I'll get an idol with your face on it and give it flowers and pigeon blood every night."

Mike colored at that, being Baptist. Forty something at least, with a groomed black beard and sunglasses hanging from his neck by a neon-green band, he was the Prime Mover of the yard's universe, spinning us into motion with his order sheets. My prayers must have climbed their way through the spheres and gotten to his ear. Ever since morning the minutes had crawled, and all I could think of was getting to quitting time and driving to The Hangout so I could pitch my woo Angela-ward.

"Where's Jimmy?" Mike said, clutching the order sheet to his chest. Jimmy popped up behind him, out of the main warehouse, where he must have been lazing in the door room. A great place for smoking, he told me once, but not for getting high, not with all those doors. Jimmy was a couple years older than me, taller, muscled, long hair straight and brown, with these little round spectacles like you see on timid townspeople in westerns. I'd been paired with him since I started at the lumberyard. After the tornado hit, they needed some extra people, and my dad was friends with a guy who went to Mike's

33

church. My first week, though, I managed to put a nail through my foot and drive over a stack of Sheetrock, and Jimmy was the only one willing to take me on. He was a general master of fuckuppery, but he'd worked at East Texas since he graduated from high school and he knew the yard. Those last were Mike's exact words.

His exact words now were, "Don't screw it up." The job was a shingle drop for two tornado houses. "Silver Linings to Greenhills and Chestnuts to Oak Ranch," Mike told us. Jimmy snatched the order sheet from him, looked it over like maybe it was a trick, then beamed at me and told me to get in the truck. Mike gave us an "All right" and headed back to his air-conditioned holy of holies. We didn't get good deliveries too often. We were always getting lost, and one time we'd scattered half our load on MLK when one of our straps came loose. But all the other guys were swamped.

We parked on the cool cement floor of the shingle warehouse, and Arturo scooted over in his forklift, glanced at the order, and said, "Pinchay my asshole." Jimmy sat there, grinning as he held his hair up in a ponytail and snapped a rubber band around it. Arturo was always shouting something obscene, and most of the guys laughed without even thinking about the translation.

"Two drops," Jimmy said to me, relishing it. "Tornado houses. And one of them in Longview."

I let myself sink into the truck's plastic leather, listened idly as Arturo put our pallets together and shouted "Pinchay my asshole" some more. Shingles were already easy because we wouldn't have to pull lumber for a load, and the Longview drop meant a good long time of getting paid for just riding around. I'd sail through the afternoon, almost nothing between me and quitting time, between me sitting here now and sitting next to Angela at The Hangout and offering to buy her a Mountain Dew.

JIMMY DROVE US THROUGH DOWNTOWN, all cracked sidewalks and empty buildings and that line of tall oil derricks they lit up for

Christmas, then over to Stone Road to skirt the tornado zone and come up along its backside.

"You got any stops you want to make?" he asked after we passed the new car wash with its imported palm trees and inflated gorilla in an Uncle Sam hat. He'd said it was a right, on long deliveries, to work in some idling.

But I didn't want the risk. I'd already measured the afternoon out in my head. Once we did our two drops and got back, it'd be four. That was a good hour to return from delivery, four. Too late to start a new job, we'd hang out eating Popsicles from the yard freezer, straightening boards and picking up scraps while the day's last minutes wound down, no worrying about getting to The Hangout in time. When I shared my dream with Jimmy— leaving out any mention of Angela, since the last thing I wanted was his needling—he said, "I got to have my stops."

"What about this. We don't fucknut around, Mike might give us some more good deliveries."

Jimmy leaned across the truck, let it glide between lanes as he reached his hand toward me. "Two stops. I'll have us back by five. I swear."

A telephone pole loomed. "Jesus, fine." I gave his hand a quick shake. "Two stops, back by five." It was the best I could do.

The thing is, the tornado had deus-ex-machinaed my life pretty well, and I was fighting to hold on to the improvements. First there was my job. The one I had before the lumberyard was at Whataburger, and I couldn't go back there. The grease coated my skin like wax, and I'd been fired anyway for leaving some meat out. I'd sat around for months, taking classes part-time at the junior college, and my parents had given me an ultimatum. I had to be out by New Year's and doing something useful, they said, so I'd decided to move to Dallas and go to the locksmith school there. My brain turned to fuzz whenever I thought too long about most things, but it'd be cool spending your day getting into other people's houses and cars. Since the tornado came and I started at the lumberyard I'd saved up about a quarter of the money I needed.

And second there was Angela. In high school I'd had only one real girlfriend. She was Church of Christ, and she kissed me with her lips closed and dumped me after a month because I kept putting my hand on her stomach and she thought I was trying to edge it somewhere else (I was). But Angela I'd already felt up once. Two weeks earlier she sat in the folding chair next to mine at The Hangout. The guy who ran The Hangout didn't charge anything—he went to Grace Church and said it was his mission for the area youth, to give us someplace to go that wasn't a cowboy bar or a random field where we might get up to who knew what. On Thursdays and Fridays the same Christian band always played, and that one night two weeks back when Angela sat next to me I caught her flipping off the singer while he was leading everybody in prayer. "He's an idiot," she said when she saw me. "He made fun of people at school and peed on my friend's car." I held her Mountain Dew for her when she went to the bathroom, and when the band took a break she told me she'd gone to high school at Pine Tree and that last year was her first year at SFA. "It sucked I missed the tornado," she said. I told her I was out there every day, delivering wood and stuff to the houses. A light turned on in her eyes. She pushed her flat brown hair behind her ears and told me she was majoring in biology, wanted to do something with frogs. I said, "Frogs are cool," and she started talking about going on a frog hunt with her science club in Davy Crockett National Forest. It was as if she'd unwrapped this hidden part of herself and was holding it out to me. I asked if she was dating anybody, offhanded-like, and she said no. So when she said she had to get home I walked her to her car. She opened her door and turned to look at me and that's when I kissed her. After we did that for about a minute I slipped my hand up her shirt and kept it there until one of the Grace volunteers watching the parking lot started beelining our way. Angela pulled back and said she had to go but that she'd see me again.

But the next night at The Hangout she ignored me and instead sat with this group of mission trippers from Jasper who'd come here to shovel in the tornado zone. A freckle-faced, lanky guy with gelled blond hair kept putting his arm around her, and she kept letting him. I couldn't figure it out. When I got her by herself, she'd barely talked to me, and it was that way every time after until last night I spotted her alone at the cake and candy table. At first I froze but then I said, "Hey," and she said, "Hey." She was holding her arm across the chest of her Scooby-Doo T-shirt, Scooby's eyes blacked out with marker, as she scratched at the eczema on her other arm. I told her I liked what she had done to her shirt and she said, "He's a dog, it's stupid, the others could still be alive now but he'd be dead." Then I said, "I haven't talked to you in forever," though it'd only been since last Friday, and she said, well, yeah, that sucked, and now she was headed back to Nacogdoches in two days for summer school. One of the Jasper mission trippers barked her name in this voice he did that made everyone laugh. She smiled at him and started leaning in that way people do when they want to leave you for somebody better. My jaw finally flopped open and "See you tomorrow?" tumbled out. She said, "Sure," and stopped scratching long enough to hold her hand up in good-bye.

Tonight was my last chance. I had to get back to the yard by five so I could be at The Hangout by six, waiting for Angela, ready to show her I was the one she wanted. That way it'd be me walking her to the parking lot when the time came, sneaking my hand up her shirt again, and seeing what happened next.

"WELL, SHIT, I guess we're late for our date," Jimmy said when we got to the first drop, over on Greenhills. Roofers crowded the top of the pink-bricked ranch house like lizards on a rock. They were drinking Cokes and lying back, eyes hooded under ballcaps. We'd done a few shingle runs before, and the first time out Jimmy had told me about roofers. "Lowest of the low," he'd said. "When a man can't get a job doing anything else, he becomes a roofer." Since then I'd always regarded roofers, and roofs, with a quiet disdain.

The head roofer came over to the truck. After we'd driven across the ruined chain-link fence and parked on the grass we'd found him sitting under a crab-apple tree, the only thing in the backyard left standing. His skin was leathered and red, and he wore a dirty denim shirt and a chewed-up Lone Star Feed hat.

"Twenty bucks and me and my partner'll put these shingles on the roof," Jimmy said, nodding at me when he said "partner."

"Done," the head roofer said, and passed Jimmy a twenty and got back under his tree. He took a Marlboro from the pack in his shirt pocket and lit up.

If the roofers didn't give us the twenty bucks we unloaded the shingles on the ground, which sucked for them. They'd have to haul the bundles up one by one on a ladder. But with the truck backed just right we only had to lift them from the bed, which was already more than halfway up the side of your basic ranch house. After he pocketed the twenty and gave me a ten, Jimmy edged the truck against the house, and then we got out.

"Go on up," Jimmy said once we'd both climbed onto the bed.

"You go up." The few other times we'd done this I'd been the one stuck on the roof. If I wasn't careful my foot could go through a soft spot, put me in a wheelchair for life if the roof was rotten enough. Mike had told me the stories himself.

"You going to sling these shingles?" Jimmy asked.

I couldn't, of course—I was too weak. Each bundle was sixty pounds. Without a word I scrabbled up over the gutter, and once I was on the roof Jimmy started handing the shingles to me. He hoisted them like they were nothing while I waddled, bent-backed, as I carried them up and down the slope of the house and dropped them wherever the roofers pointed. They didn't get up, just nodded and grunted. As I walked back to fetch the next bundle, my arms floated up in release and I'd look out at the mile-long tornado cut that ran through town, scabbed over here and there with fresh plywood and timber, dotted with trash piles and teams of volunteers in the neon-colored shirts donated by the TV station over in Tyler. Then I'd pick up the next bundle and forget about the tornado as I strained and breathed little breaths and prayed I wouldn't make a fool of myself before I dumped the sucker. On the roof's far slope, where the plywood hadn't been replaced, it was harder to find the rafters, and my third trip over I missed one. My foot sank into the plywood—a soft spot, rotted to sponge. This was it. Thinking of Angela, the three minutes of her I'd had and all the minutes I wanted, I eased my weight to my other foot, still balanced on a rafter. The roofer watching me let out a guzzling laugh. I wobbled, then got myself clear, and once both feet were settled I tossed the shingles before the roofer could point. We only had a few bundles left and each trip back I eyed the divot and moved my feet in straight lines along the rafters I'd found. Soon we'd finished. The roofers began to cuss and rise. Before I got off the roof they already had the nail guns going, the bright new chestnut shingles spreading up from the eaves.

WHEN THE TORNADO HAD COME, back in April, I was at the junior college, on the top floor of Pfaff Hall waiting for my history class. The siren we always heard on the second Wednesday of every month blared, and at first I thought it was an idiot cop pulling a prank. But then an announcement echoed down the cinder-block halls: a tornado had touched down and we had to get to the bottom floor, away from glass. A sudden giddiness rattled the air. The juco profs stationed themselves at spaced points and waved us forward, as if they'd trained for it, and at the end of the hall Franciosa James, who I'd shared a table with in fourth-grade homeroom, shouted, "Gonna motherfucking storm up in here." People near him laughed. "I ain't making no joke."

Franciosa's words were the true signal. Low-grade panic kicked through me, and I fought my way toward the stairs, weaving around others. Just before the stairwell, though, I got blocked by three girls whose tank-topped, salon-toasted skin I'd contemplated all semester. They held each other as they walked, the one in the middle bawling. Temporarily forfeiting my panic, I reached out to put a hand on her. With everything upended, who knew what might happen? But a guy in a camo shirt elbowed himself between us. The bulk of his thick, broad body muffled what I'd started saying to the girl, about it being okay, and I had to listen to him show off. He said he'd walk right now over to the Show Room for a shot if he could get some company, and one of the girls chuckled. I gave up and downstairs I sat an extra length from the nearest person. Death, I meet thee alone, I said to myself, thinking it was from a poem in high school. I didn't really believe I was going to die, I just liked the charge of it, like everyone else.

A giant girl in shiny basketball shorts, curly hair sweat-plastered to her head, stared at her cell phone as texts came in and called out to everyone that the tornado had crossed Dudley Road. Then the power went out and the bawling girl screamed. In school they'd told us a tornado was supposed to sound like a freight train, but I didn't hear anything. We all sat there in silence, except the guy in the camo shirt, who for no reason burst out laughing a couple of times, maniacal. Twenty minutes later a janitor came in and said we could get up, the tornado was gone. It had veered just after Dudley and sliced through another part of town.

For a moment disappointment seeped through the hall, then we rallied. Everyone tried their cell phones, but the tower must have been down, so we filed out of the building and while some went to their cars I settled in with the rest—the three girls among them—who walked under the now-calm sky to look for destruction. We headed east, where the janitor and sweaty-haired girl's reports had last placed the tornado, and at Henderson Boulevard we found a police barricade already put up. A hushed crowd had gathered along it, bristling with arms that wheeled about at the whims of greedy, pointing fingers. Across from the barricade the doughnut shop had folded in on itself, its refrigerator of milks tilting out what remained of the front door, the cartons spoiling in the sun. I could only muster a whispered "Holy shit" as I marveled. Half a block up the famous barbecue place had vanished into a pile, its blue vans picked up and sprinkled across the street. Paramedics were there, ministering to people with cuts. Beyond, in the neighborhood that spread from behind the strip of restaurants, splintery twists of wood curled up out of the ground, the remains of trees, and the houses looked like knocked-out drunks, windows empty and black, bits of everything vomited everywhere, glass, mail, china, pictures, stuffed animals, appliances large and small. A police cruiser was parked at the head of the street, lights flashing, and at some of the houses people had come into their yards. It was like looking at zoo animals in their habitats. Beside me a knot of men estimated death counts. Ten, twenty. One fevered guy in a green Subway shirt said it'd be a hundred at least. Some police had stopped in for footlong tunas, and that's what he'd heard, a hundred, and then he'd clocked out and left to come see. The number jittered through me. I looked around for the three girls, hoping I could be the one to tell them, but they were off who knew where.

As it happened, by the end of the day the count had dropped to one, a ninety-year-old man, Earl Vancey, who hardly anybody knew. Didn't go to any church, sat by himself each morning at the Circle Café, same coffee and oatmeal, same denim shirt. When the tornado came he'd crouched in his bathtub and the wall above him had fallen in. Everyone said they were relieved it was only the one, a blessing, especially with him being so old. But now the president and the governor wouldn't come, and there'd be no movie stars or other famous people to escort through the wreckage. We were lucky to make the scroll on the bottom of the twenty-four-hour news. Still, the destruction was enough to attract Baptist men's clubs, who roved the tornado site wielding chain saws, and mission groups with their crates of bottled water and sacks of donated clothes. It was enough to get me this job and Angela in my arms.

AFTER THE GREENHILLS DROP Jimmy looped us back to 259, but instead of keeping straight on toward Longview he turned left on 31. "Stop one, need to swing by the house," he said.

We'd never before gone home while on the clock. Pulled over for tacos, lingered in convenience stores, taken long routes, sure, but this was a line we were crossing. Still, I hadn't bargained for a veto, so I kept my mouth shut, crossed my fingers, and soothed myself with images of me at The Hangout, right on time.

I didn't know where Jimmy lived and was surprised when he took the ramp onto 135 and we drove past the oilfield shops that lined the edge of town. Out here there was no trace of the tornado, but it was ugly all the same. The road was four-lane, a big highway in the middle of nowhere, and after we got to the last of five identical mustard-colored buildings with their attendant gravel lots, we pulled into a potholed driveway. Houses floated around us in a sea of tall grass. They sat on metal beams, hides of shagged tarpaper gathered about grayed, termite-ridden wood. Jimmy drove past them to a yard of smoothly packed dirt where a house in only slightly better shape than the others squatted on cement-block feet.

"My dad buys them," Jimmy said, when he noticed me looking back at the houses in the field. "He's going to turn them into lake cabins."

He leaped out of the truck and, passing the front porch, started climbing through a window. I didn't want to think about why, and staring out at the field of houses I ignored his legs wiggling over the sill and let my mind drift to the moonflesh beneath Angela's shirt. I struggled with my inadequate map, itched at not knowing how much ground had been lost to the guy from Jasper. Then a banging on the hood set my heart knocking in my chest. Jimmy. He opened my door and started pushing me toward the steering wheel.

"You're going to drive," he said. He'd shoved me halfway across the cab and now lifted himself up to where I'd been sitting, pulled a joint out from his pocket, and punched the truck's lighter with his thumb. "I'm going to smoke."

"We both have so much to live for," I said. To no avail—one last push had me behind the wheel. I sucked at driving the trucks and I didn't have my CDL. But the afternoon tugged, and fighting Jimmy would mean losing more time. I did some active visualization, me returned to the yard safe, then started the truck, backed around to straighten us up, and pretended not to be frightened as I got us past all those houses and onto 135, shifting through the gears and popping the stick until the engine stopped making its horrible grinding noises.

A mile gone, the lighter released and Jimmy grabbed it and touched it to the end of his joint. "Snow cones," he said. "That's stop two."

THE SNOW-CONE STAND JIMMY WANTED was on the edge of the Family Dollar parking lot in Sabine. As I drove us there the truck kept losing its smooth gear, bucking and heaving until I tamed it with blind shoves of the stick. Meanwhile, Jimmy preened: he took off his glasses, undid his ponytail, combed his fingers through his hair, all with the joint pinched between his lips. When I at last got us to the stand he said, "Keep going, keep going," until we were clear on the other side of the lot. I lurched the truck to a stop in a row of empty spaces, but Jimmy didn't shift from his seat. Instead, he pulled a five from his pocket, passed it to me, and told me to get him a pink lemon.

"You're not getting out?"

"Does it look like I'm getting out?" Then, calm again, "Get yourself something, too."

"Okay, but you're driving after this."

"Fine. Just let me finish." He held up the end of his joint.

I walked across the asphalt toward the stand, a cube of slapped-together plywood painted white. On each side, above red, yellow, and blue circles, stenciled letters spelled "Sno-Cone." Inside the stand a blond girl leaned against the back counter and paged through a magazine covered with exposé photos of some celebrity's fat-curdled belly. A donation canister for the tornado victims sat beneath the list of flavors.

"One pink lemon, one blue coconut," I said, putting Jimmy's five on the counter. The girl flicked her eyes at me, smacked her gum, and repeated, "One pink lemon, one blue coconut," as if they were the two most boring flavors ever. She dropped the magazine on the counter and took two cups from the stack beside her, then turned around and filled them with shaved ice. The stand was raised up so that my eyes pointed directly at her butt. I envisioned myself somehow lodged in the tuck of denim between cheek and thigh.

"Is that Jimmy in that truck?" the girl said, back still to me as she stood at the jugs of syrups and pumped the cones with color.

"Which Jimmy?"

"You know which Jimmy," she said.

"Well," I said, "within the infinite possibilities of Jimmys, that very well could be the Jimmy you want it to be."

She set the snow cones down. "Whatever. You can tell that infinite Jimmy to stop bothering me. Next time I see him I'm going to slap him upside his head."

"I'll pass that on to the Jimmys I know," I said.

She picked up a rag and gave me a slit-eyed scowl. "Whatever it is you want, you ain't getting it." Then she turned around and ran the rag along the shelf beneath the syrups, where drips collected from the gummed and crusted nozzles. "But you can go right ahead and stare at my ass again."

I blushed, didn't say anything, and took the snow cones back to the truck. Jimmy was slouched in the driver's seat, his head just above the window, watching the girl. I gave him his pink lemon, told him what she'd said, and for a few seconds we studied her together.

"She dispenses nectar," Jimmy said, and scraped his teeth over the syrupy ice, slow and reverent. Sure, he had ape muscles and went to parties where people got drunk and naked, but he read fantasy novels, too.

After he tipped the last of the snow cone into his mouth he put the truck in gear and guided us to the street. Loose asphalt crackled beneath our tires. I ran over one more time what I'd decided to say to Angela that night. First I would ask her if she wanted a Mountain Dew, and when I brought her one I would put my hand on her arm and look her in the eyes and say she might be going back to Nacogdoches and I might be moving to Dallas someday, but now that we lived in a world with tornadoes what did that matter, we had tonight. Then I'd stay quiet for a moment and she wouldn't say anything, just nod and let me take her to her car. And that would lead to other nights. Nacogdoches was only an hour away. I could drive there at least once a week.

It was four o'clock when we got to Longview.

"I need something to eat," Jimmy said. He looked at me, his eyes gone soft. It was the first he'd spoken since we left the snow-cone stand.

"Two stops is two stops," I said.

"I'll be quick. Please. You do something good, something good will happen to you. Rule of the universe."

"Ha."

"Your call," Jimmy said. Then he smiled. "Angela Grimes."

An acid shudder flashed through my stomach. "You know about Angela?"

Jimmy pretended not to hear me, slapped his palms on the steering wheel to the drum solo being spat out by 97X.

"What do you know?"

The solo finished, he said, "I'm too hungry and upset to remember."

I looked at the green numbers of the clock. We could still make five if we hurried. "You'll be quick?"

"You won't even see me eat."

Jimmy drove us to the Waffle Shoppe, a twenty-four-hour place on the corner of 80 and McCann with a sign that had a waffle the shape of Texas on it, a big pat of melting butter where Waco would be. Counting minutes, I'd suggested McDonald's, but Jimmy had said he didn't believe in McDonald's, and then he'd repeated Angela's name. Inside we took one of the stunted booths next to the counter, and when the brown-shirted waitress came by Jimmy ordered a jalapeño omelet. She looked at me and I said I didn't want anything, but Jimmy winked at her and told her to bring me a pecan waffle.

"So that girl at the snow-cone stand," Jimmy said when the waitress left. "Beth. Last weekend I was at this party and her friend got me into a room and pulled down her pants and was like, 'Fuck me,' and so I did. And then Beth comes into the room all like, 'What are you doing fucking my friend on my little sister's bed?'"

"What's this got to do with Angela?"

Jimmy blinked at me. "Nothing. I just needed to clear out my own shit. Beth's the one I want and she's just mean to me."

The waitress returned, and plates and silverware clattered onto our table. Jimmy gave the woman his wide grin, said thanks, and sliced the end off his omelet and shoved it into his mouth.

"So," I said. "You've got food in you now."

"Oh, yeah, sweet little Angela. We go back." He forked in more omelet. "Her brother throws big parties in Pine Tree. I was at one last night and she told me you loved up on her."

I poured syrup on my waffle, let it pool over the edges.

"She said, hey, you know this guy, I think he works where you work, he felt me up in the parking lot, and I said I bet he was gentle, and then she said she was about to piss her panties and went in the bathroom. She had her frogs with her after some guy had snuck in her room and tried to lick them."

"Did she tell you why she's been ignoring me? Because she's been ignoring me."

Jimmy shrugged. "She's always been one of those secret shy girls. You know, you think she's all cool talking but then she gets spooked." He licked mashed omelet off his lips. "I can tell you something, though. She's primed. I've got a nose for it. You need to get your finger wet."

He held his own finger up and danced it in a slow twirl. I slid down in my booth. Its seat was stitched with duct tape, the stuffing a memory, and the coils pushed back like they wanted to spring me out.

"It'll be you or somebody else, and if it's you you'll hook her."

A dizzy tingle skittered up my nerves. I darted an eye to the tables around us, empty except for one, a guy with a trucker's beard and a folded-up newspaper. Jimmy's plate was empty now, speckled with yellow grease and jalapeño seeds. On my own plate my waffle remained untouched, a soggy moon.

"We should go," I said, and Jimmy turned his twirling finger at the waitress and asked for the check.

AT THE OAK RANCH DEVELOPMENT we drove past staked-off lots of plowed-over red clay and cul-de-sacs of two-by-four pine skeletons until we came to a small herd of near-finished houses. A second tornado, in the same storm, had touched down here, but it was smaller than the one in our town and had only scraped along the empty streets, tearing up roofs and breaking windows. Jimmy did his routine with the head roofer, a guy in a clean buttoned shirt and matching ball cap stitched with his company's name. The man looked at the two of us, smiled, and told us he'd keep his twenty.

"Fuck him," Jimmy said. He climbed up onto the bed and flung the pallet as far as he could from the house. "He wants to lug them, we'll make him lug them. Get over there."

I didn't mind losing the twenty. Unloading the shingles on the ground was faster than putting them on the roof, especially once you got into a rhythm. It was four thirty now, and since Jimmy's revelations at the Waffle Shoppe I'd had to do several of the slow-exhale exercises I'd learned in seventh-grade gym.

I hustled to the pallet. Jimmy threw the shingles down and I lined them up as they fell, pulling back as the next bundle soared toward me. Our bodies turned into simple, timed machines, I let my mind float to The Hangout. I wasn't asking Angela if she wanted a Mountain Dew, I was just buying it for her, showing her nobody knew her like I did. Then I was telling her about living in the world with tornadoes. Her face was pointed toward mine, lips soft and open and sugared from her drink. If the stuff about the tornado didn't work, I'd tell her I knew where the old man had died and that I could take her there, anything to get me with her. I wondered if she'd be wearing the same bra. The one before had been this thin cotton, with a useless bow between the cups that I wanted to untie and keep in my pants.

"Shit!" Jimmy yelled.

I looked back. A bundle of shingles was midair, meteoring toward me. I'd faltered out of rhythm, and the bundle's corner caught my side, a deep punch beneath my ribs, then spun to the ground. I bent over, held my breath as tears gathered at my eyes and a bruise knuckled to life beneath my skin.

"Fucktard," Jimmy said. "You awake?"

"Yeah," I said.

"Then go pick those shingles up."

The bundle had ripped open, silver shingles fanned out. Ignoring the throbs around my kidney, I scooped the shingles together and dumped them on the pallet. Jimmy hurled the rest of the shingles down and I fenced my brain, kept it away from that bow, and didn't break the rhythm. By the time we were finished and sitting in the truck my side only ached a little and I was feeling pretty good. We'd get back just after five and I could still be showered and at The Hangout by six.

Jimmy drove us down McCann, then 31. No more wandering, we were headed directly home. Honks blared around us from the highway as Jimmy told me about some show he'd watched where wolves captured people's souls. In the rearview mirror I saw we'd forgotten to tighten one of the straps. It whipped out off the side of the truck like a devil's tail.

TEN MINUTES AFTER FIVE and the yard was already dormant, that sweet time when the start of the next day was at its farthest. The sun hung high above the far sheds, a lone white dot. The other trucks had been pulled in for the night, angled one next to the other, like children put to bed, and I had to get out and unlock the gate. As I swung it open I thought about Angela and my hand and how the two would soon join.

I had gotten the gate wide enough for the truck when a door slammed, echoing out into the yard and jostling the image of me and Angela in The Hangout's parking lot. I looked around, caught Mike shooting toward me from the office, and at the sight of him my stomach flipped over on itself like a badly turned pancake. His face was red, and his throat made a grinding noise, like some possessed person in the movies. I clung to the gate and heard Jimmy brake the truck behind me.

Mike's glare jumped from me to Jimmy and back again before he got his throat to working. "You took the wrong dadgummed shingles to the wrong dadgummed house! I just got a call from Greenhills. The customer came out of her house and looked up and what did she see? Chestnut shingles. What did she order? Silver Lining."

I stood there, my fogged brain not computing what this meant for me, The Hangout awaiting.

But after another quick bout of throat grinding, Mike said, "You want to keep this job, you better get out there right now and fix it." The little hopes I'd been tending popped and crumpled beneath my skin. We'd have to load new shingles for the Longview house, then get the shingles we'd dropped there and take them to Greenhills—we wouldn't be done until eight, and by then it'd be the Jasper guy with his arm around Angela, getting his hands wherever he could, making dates to see her in Nacogdoches.

"How about early tomorrow—" I began, but Mike turned his red face on me and I swallowed whatever else it was I was going to say. Jimmy started bitching, then gunned the truck and told me to come on. I gave him my chained-dog look, like just step closer and I'll maul you. All the hours I'd gotten through and we'd fucked up before we even knew it. Good-bye, Angela. Then I dragged myself around the front of the truck and up into the cab. I mean, Jesus, but it would take a dozen tornadoes to get me the life I wanted.

THE DON'S CINNAMON

WHEN BURKE RETURNED TO HIS ROOMS from his morning visit to the sea baths, Fernandita, his maid, was shaking the bugs out of his mosquito net. He lived in cramped quarters, on the second floor of an old mansion between the wharves and the post office. The mansion's ground floor was given over to a molasses warehouse, and its top floors had been cut into apartments. Burke occupied one of these, an old bedchamber in the back of the building that was partitioned into three rooms and looked over the harbor. One room served as his bedroom, its neighbor as his small study and parlor, and the third room, barely a closet, was Fernandita's.

"Your food is on the desk," Fernandita said, giving the net one more vigorous shake before sweeping the loosed mosquitoes and other insects onto a scrap of newspaper. A skinny, toothless, yellow-skinned woman past middle age, Fernandita was Burke's only companion in the city.

Inspecting his breakfast, Burke picked a green beetle from his eggs and tossed it into the grate, where Fernandita had lit a small flame, then he sat and ate as he read again the letter he'd received from Don Hernán Vargas y Lombilla. My business is most delicate, Don Hernán had written, giving no further clue to the nature of his problem. Burke hoped for a challenge, and let his mind wander once more, imagining all the possible conundrums the don might present him.

He was at the start of his life, twenty-two, a free gentleman of color who had left his home in the lower Brazos not a year before. His mother had been a slave, his father a Texas sugar planter. Burke had come to Havana after his father died, freeing him, as he thought that here he might make use of his Spanish and his knowledge of the sugar business. But his various inquiries at those trading houses open to negroes met only with vague promises of later openings, and within four months he was down to his last pennies. It was then he'd read an account of a mystery baffling the city: a nun in the Convent of Santa Clarita had been poisoned, yet she seemed to have no enemies and the walls of the convent were most secure. Puzzling over the story and the details of the nun's life, Burke had soon figured out how it must have been done. The dentist who visited the convent had mixed her toothpowder with arsenic. Burke wrote the captain-general with the solution, and the dentist, taken by the police, confessed to the crime. Unbeknownst to the nun, she had been named in the will of a wealthy coffee grower, an uncle, and were she to die the legacy was to pass to a distant cousin—the man who'd bribed the dentist.

At a loss for income and facing mounting debts, Burke had seen then how he might support himself. After the Case of the Poisoned Toothpowder he was approached with another, and soon Habaneros burdened with seemingly insoluble problems were calling on him in his rooms at least once a week. He took each case offered him, stringing together enough money to pay his creditors as he swiftly established a reputation for uncommon subtlety and skill.

AFTER HE FINISHED HIS BREAKFAST, Burke was fetched by one of the don's *volantas*. It was driven by a negro postilion and fitted out with soft leather seats, a Turkish rug, and, lodged in a teak case, a brass lorgnette for observing passengers in other carriages. As he rode, Burke tried the lorgnette but, feeling foolish, soon put it away and sat for the rest of the trip with his hands in his lap. Within twenty-five minutes he was delivered to a sprawling estate near the top of the Jesús del Monte. The postilion stopped at the front door, and Burke alighted and was immediately led by another negro down a marble-floored hallway, into a courtyard with a tinkling fountain encircled by orange trees, and then into the don's office, where gilt-framed ancestors stared down from the walls and old account ledgers filled the bookshelves. For fifteen minutes Burke sat alone. Then, at ten precisely, the don strode into the room. Burke had worn his dark coat, white waistcoat, and white drill trousers, the uniform Havana fashion demanded of its gentlemen, but Don Hernán, a stout man with gray, slicked hair and a waxed imperial, was in his silk dressing gown. He snapped at the liveried slave, who then stepped forward and presented two plates piled with eggs and the plump red sausages they'd lately begun selling in the markets. "French sausages" they were called—a bid, Burke suspected, to justify their expense.

"No, thank you, I'm quite full," Burke said, refusing his plate with an apologetic smile. The don snapped again at the slave, and the slave transferred Burke's servings to the don's plate.

Don Hernán did not speak as he ate, and Burke remained silent. He watched as the don cut each sausage into three pieces and shoved the pieces into his mouth, grease dribbling into his imperial. Now that he was here, Burke was nervous about the meeting. One of the island's wealthiest sugar planters, Don Hernán held more sway in Havana than any other creole and could, with a single whisper, ruin Burke's career before it had even begun. A man in his sixties who looked younger than his years—he was childless and a carouser—he was known to be fickle and demanding. Whatever the don's request, Burke couldn't afford to fail him.

When the don finished eating, he shoved the plate away, dabbed at his lips, then lit a cigar. Once he had the cigar going, he eased back in his chair. "A month ago," he said, "the manager of my Santo Cristo estate sent up a load of fruit along with two slaves to work in the house. The next day the mules, still bearing the fruit, were found grazing in a field off the Infanta highway, three miles outside the city. The two slaves were gone without a trace."

The don paused. Burke held himself erect in his seat, but unease rippled through him. So far he'd avoided any cases that touched on slaves.

"That was a month ago. A week ago I lost my treasure, my Marcita." The don fumbled in the pocket of his gown and pulled out a gilt-framed daguerreotype and passed it to Burke. "My cinnamon," the don said. "She is most precious to me."

As Burke examined the photograph, his palms sweated a little. A mulatta in a muslin dress, her hair curled and tied with ribbons, stared out from the photographer's painted landscape—a wooded hill, a distant temple. Her face was soft-featured, her eyes heavy-lidded, her mouth drawn into a coquette's half smile. Her skin, from the picture's tint, indeed seemed a bronze, cinnamon hue. Burke gave the picture back to the don, who returned it to his pocket.

"I'm not the only one with losses. It has been the talk of the Planters' Club for weeks. Don Sancho is missing four slaves, Don Nicasio is missing five. And these just from the city. It seems to be the season of runaways." He took a puff of his cigar, let out the smoke. "I have put her description in the papers with the offer of a reward, and I've had two of the city's best slave hunters watching for her. All for nothing. So now I try you." He put his hand on his desk and leaned forward. "I want you to find Marcita. It is hard, without my cinnamon here to comb my hair and soothe me." In that moment, the man seemed truly distraught.

In Burke's mind, a vision of himself stood, bowed stiffly, and pronounced that on his conscience he must refuse. But Don Hernán could ruin him. He hesitated as long as he could, his thoughts a fog. Then Don Hernán coughed impatiently and Burke lowered his eyes and said, "I am at your service."

AFTER HE AGREED TO TAKE THE CASE, a cold dizziness bloomed beneath Burke's chest. He fought it as best he could with procedure. In questioning the don and several of the other slaves, Burke learned that Marcita had disappeared in the Calle O'Reilly while marketing in the company of two slave boys, Domingo and Miércoles. They were out on an errand, so Burke arranged to have the boys meet him in the city at five. Then he made an inspection of Marcita's quarters. She lived in a small room near the kitchens. One wall was decorated with an advertisement for an Italian soprano who had appeared on the stage two years before, and another with a collection of Honradez cigarette labels from a series depicting the progress of a *pollo,* a fop, from prince of the ball to beggar. Another series of labels, these for a Villargas brand, lay on her bedside table. They showed each of the islands of the Antilles as ladies, Cuba regal and bedecked with pearls and tobacco leaves, sprinkling sugar onto a globe, Santo Domingo a weeping negress with torn skirts. In a plain earthen jar Burke found a bundle of feathers and dried leaves, of the kind you could buy from the guinea women in the night markets for good luck, and beneath a loose tile he discovered a burlap sack filled with coins. He paused over this last item, wondering what might have compelled Marcita to forget the sack when she ran. Perhaps it meant she had fled on impulse. Then he left, sitting once more in the don's high-wheeled carriage, his observations pressed against the front of his mind to stanch any seepings of guilt.

BURKE DIDN'T RETURN TO THE CALLE DEL SOL, where the old mansion that housed his rooms stood, until past one. The midday heat had already blanketed the city, and after a light lunch he isolated himself in his bedroom and rested. At three he woke to the call of a plantain vendor in the street below. The city was not yet stirring—the plantain vendor's cry was the only noise that came from outside—and he moved to his study and remained there while the heat lifted. The effort to quash any notion of himself as a slave hunter had failed and he tried to compose a letter to Don Hernán, regretting that he could not finish the case and begging the don that it would not cost him his esteem, but he could not find the right words. No matter the phrasing, the don would be disappointed and insulted. Besides, Burke had already given part of his fee to Fernandita to pay off the butcher. He decided he had no choice now, and when his clock struck four forty-five he rose and left his rooms and went out the courtyard gate to keep his appointment with the don's two slaveboys.

The sky was high and blue, and, with the worst of the day's heat finally past, the city had spilled once more into the streets. Gentlemen in broad-brimmed straw hats walked together speaking of business, Capuchins delivered alms, a company of soldiers marched in seersucker uniforms, a lottery ticket seller cried out that his numbers were blessed. Burke had to pass through this throng as he crossed the Plaza de Armas, skirting Ferdinand VII on his pedestal, then going along the university walls and into the Calle O'Reilly. There he found the street, as usual, blocked with *volantas*. Pale ladies shaded by umbrellas sat in the carriages while shopkeepers came out of their shops to present them with their wares. Burke picked his way around them and after a block found the two boys waiting for him by the sweetshop. They were dressed in the don's blue livery and engrossed in a game of punching each other in the arm. Burke introduced himself, then took them aside from the bustle and asked them to show him where Marcita had disappeared.

Miércoles, who was the older of the two boys, pointed toward a row of shops past the Calle Habana intersection. "She tole us to get some oysters, so we were loadin up the baskets, and when we done, she was gone."

Domingo, the smaller and darker skinned of the two, nodded.

"And you saw nothing?"

Miércoles said he'd been watching the road while he held his basket and hadn't seen her come back past. He thought she'd gone farther up the street.

Burke put his hands on the boys' shoulders and walked them closer to the shops. The first shop off the Calle Habana intersection was the oyster stall, and next was the narrow stall of the Gallitos brand's tobacco shop, and after that a bookseller's. A corpulent, red-bearded fellow was dressing the Gallitos window with rolls of cigarettes. The prices were absurdly high, even for Havana standards, and the shop looked empty; Pedroso y Compañia, manufacturers of the Gallitos brand, had gone bankrupt two months before, and it appeared the new owners would do no better. Next door, however, the bookseller was doing a brisk business selling copies of *David Copperfield*. He sat beside his crate and handed copies up to the ladies who rode past, catching their coins in his palm. Burke asked what the boys had done after Marcita disappeared, and Miércoles told him that they waited a half hour then returned to the don's villa on the horse trolley.

"And you didn't worry?"

"Not on Tuesdays," Domingo said.

Miércoles glared at Domingo, and Domingo clapped his hand over his lips.

"Ah, so she met someone on Tuesdays," Burke said. "Who?"

Miércoles looked at his feet. "Her love man," he said. Then he pinched Domingo until the smaller boy yelped.

Burke had the boys lead him to the lover's rooms. They took him up the block to the Calle Compostela, turned right and past the Church of Santa Catalina, then walked north two blocks, then turned again, toward the city walls. They stopped finally before a dingy, mud-daubed building in the Calle Villegas. Burke asked which room was the lover's, and the boys pointed toward a window on the top floor, the one farthest to the right. Leaving the boys in the street, Burke walked into the courtyard, up the stairs, and onto the interior veranda, found the lover's door, and knocked. There was no answer. Beside the door someone had tacked a piece of paperboard that read Enrique López, Merchant. A grand title, Burke thought, for one who lived in one of the poorest buildings in the city. He waited and knocked again. Still no answer. Burke wasn't sure what to do. At last he took his card, wrote Marcita's name on it, and slid it under the door. Then he came out and walked the boys back to the sweetshop, where he bought them sugar sticks and sent them on their way.

THE CASE, it seemed, was shut. Marcita had absconded with her lover. That was an explanation he could give Don Hernán. Tomorrow morning he could send him the man's name. Surely that would be enough. He'd refuse to track the two further, to clamp Marcita in irons.

He sat in a café and drank a horchata. As he sipped the cool drink and watched the street, he remembered what his mother had told him the last time he saw her. Burke had been brought up in the plantation house by his father, taught to read the books in the library, and allowed to range freely over his father's land with his own gun to shoot birds in the marshes. There was no white wife— Burke's father had been a bachelor—and so Burke's mother was allowed to come spend evenings with him every month or so. "You make me proud," she'd told him, pulling on the sleeves of his little velvet coat. He was eleven. "And you're gonna keep making me proud. You're gonna grow up and do good and be good to people." She'd died two weeks later, when fever spread up the bayous.

When he'd stumbled on detective work, he'd thought again of his mother's words. It was all he'd wanted, to do good, and here was his chance. He eased troubled minds, rooted out wrongs.

Later, hours past supper, Burke lay down to sleep and found he couldn't. A thought had come to him and refused to leave. Sending the lover's name to the don—would it be any different from putting the irons on Marcita himself?

THE NEXT MORNING, Fernandita brought him coffee and a buttered roll and set them on his desk. As he ate the roll, he watched the tangle of masts outside his window and considered whether he could write the letter. Fernandita was scraping ash out of the grate.

"What sort of man must I be," he asked her, "to trap this girl for pay?"

He did not typically consult Fernandita on matters beyond the day's marketing, but he was desperate. He'd barely slept, his mind brimming with the image of himself delivering a chained Marcita to the don's office.

"A practical man," Fernandita began, but was interrupted by the cry of one of the city's rumor sellers in the street below. In the man's singsong Burke had caught the word *murder*. He leaned his head out the window, spotted the seller, a beggar in a tattered hat. The man had started up his cry again when Burke whistled and asked, "What murder?"

The beggar looked up. "Toss me a roll and a real and I'll tell you."

Burke did so, and the man said some soldiers had been drinking in a field outside town when they found a slave's body.

"Where?" Burke asked.

"Between the Paseo de Tacón and the railroad."

"Man or woman?"

The beggar shrugged.

Burke crossed the study to the door, and once in the street he hailed a carriage, a hack with a negro driver. It was a stretch, but it gave him an excuse to delay writing the don. "Take me to the Paseo de Tacón," Burke said, and the driver began weaving out of the city, moving his carriage skillfully through the crowds.

Twenty minutes later they came to a field scattered with soldiers. An army lieutenant and two government clerks stood at the back of the field, beside a grove of bushes, smoking, and behind them an orderly was brewing coffee. When Burke got out of the hack he made for them. As he approached, one of the clerks, a short man with gray sideburns and the flat, bland face of a sheep, stepped forward.

"You have no business here," he said.

"I might," Burke answered, and offered the man his card. "I'm in the employ of Don Hernán Vargas y Lombillo."

The man broke into a grin and thumped the card with his forefinger. "I know of you," he said. "You're called the negrito. My name is Galván. You are most welcome."

Burke stifled a wince. He was not fond of the appellation the city had given him. "Thank you. I only want to see the body."

"Ah, that is a problem," Galván said, looking across the field, where soldiers and policemen in brown holland uniforms were beating the grass with sticks. "We haven't yet found the body. All we have is the head."

"Only the head," Burke said, then asked, "may I look?"

"Of course." Galván spread his arm. "It's just over there." He pointed to the grove. "Forgive me if I don't join you. I've had my fill."

Burke thanked the man, then went over to the grove, parted the branches, and saw the head. His heart sank. The head belonged to a dark-skinned man with a scar running from his forehead to his cheek. He'd not admitted it to himself, but he'd hoped to find Marcita here and so be free of his burden. He thought to leave, but then decided to take a closer look. As he knelt and examined the head, all the noises behind him—the lieutenant's guffaw, the policemen's and soldiers' complaints, the *sush* of their sticks against the grass—fell away. The head lay faceup, the skin ragged with gore along the neck where it had been severed. But no blood had drained onto the soil, a fact Burke found curious. The head must have been severed at some other place. He looked at the eyes, felt a chill when their gaze seemed to catch him, and wondered why the body was not here as well. He stood and went over to Galván.

"What's near here?" he asked.

"Only the railroad tracks, the woods, the field, and those factories."

Burke looked around the area. The tracks divided the field from the woods, and the factories—three of them, a nail factory, a cigarette factory, a snuff mill—stood on the field's western end. Any evidence of the killer's path had been destroyed by the soldiers beating through the field.

He had no business with the murder, but he found himself interested. "Would you mind sending me word once the body is found?"

"It'd be a pleasure," Galván answered.

WHEN BURKE RETURNED TO HIS ROOMS, he found a note under his door. Fernandita was out, marketing for his supper, and the note was from Marcita's lover. He'd come by, hoping to speak.

After leaving his card at the lover's room, Burke had both worried and hoped that the man would flee, if he hadn't already, that he would take Marcita from her hiding place and disappear. But instead the lover had come seeking him out? Burke stuffed the note in his pocket and turned around, going back out into the courtyard and through the streets toward the man's dismal building.

When Burke arrived and knocked on the lover's door, the man answered and beckoned him inside. He was a mulatto, at least two shades lighter than Burke and twenty years his senior. His cheeks and nose were covered with freckles, and he had a high, wide brow. The flesh beneath his eyes was puffed, the eyes themselves red.

"Please, sit," the lover said, clearing a crate filled with tins from a chair. Burke did so and looked about the cramped room. Its walls were stained a pale yellow, and aside from another chair the only other piece of furniture was a couch whose crimson velvet had been worn to bare pink patches. He was about to ask the lover about Marcita when the man, unable to contain himself, shot out, "Tell me where she is. I beg you. Tell me what you know. Tell me anything."

Burke, alarmed, straightened in his chair. "I was hoping," he said, "you'd be able to do that for me."

"But I thought she'd sent you!" Enrique said, then pleaded, "why torture me with your note?"

"I'm trying to find her," Burke said.

Enrique was silent a moment. Then something seemed to catch. "Why?" he asked. A nervousness entered his voice. "Who hired you? Was it Don Hernán?"

"I'm under his employ, but he didn't—"

"He knows?" At that he went to the window. A gauzy sheet hung there, luffing in the wind. "Oh, no no no."

"I can assure you Don Hernán knows nothing," Burke said, "and I can further assure you that he will learn nothing. You are safe. I'm charged only to find Marcita. That I will do, and nothing else."

Enrique pulled back the curtain and looked out. Then he stepped back toward Burke. "I love her," he said. "When she is free, we're going to move to Santo Domingo, away from the don, away from this island. I've been saving money to help her. See?" He offered Burke one of the tins in the crate. A crowned cow stared out from its label, which touted the contents as superior butter. "I sell this, for my living, for her. I was waiting for her last Tuesday. We were going to have an hour. But then she didn't show. I worried. I thought the don had found out. Then I saw the notices the don put in the paper, and I thought maybe she had run."

Burke's mind began to leap with what Enrique had told him. "You were waiting for her on Tuesday?" he asked.

"Yes, yes," Enrique said.

"Where, exactly?"

"At the corner of O'Reilly and Compostela."

"And you kept a hard watch for her?"

"I always do."

Burke rose, relief breaking through him like morning sun. She wasn't a runaway—she had truly disappeared. "Thank you," he said. Then, without another word, he went to the door.

"Is that all?" Enrique asked, still standing by the window and staring after Burke.

"It is enough."

BURKE WALKED DIRECTLY to the Calle O'Reilly. There, halfway between the Habana and Compostela intersections, he planted himself in the center of the street. He looked eastward, toward the intersection where Miércoles and Domingo had waited, O'Reilly and Habana. Then he pivoted and looked westward, toward the intersection where Enrique had kept a sharp lookout, O'Reilly and Compostela. Between these two lookouts, one at either entrance to the block, Marcita had vanished.

On the left side of the street were the oyster shop, the bookseller's, and the tobacco shop he'd seen before, and farther on a linen shop and a silversmith's. On the right stood a tea shop, a music shop, a large shop selling glassware, and a perfumery. There was nothing strange about the block. The shops were all elegant, glass-fronted establishments that catered to the city's gentry. They had preposterous names like The Empress Eugénie (the perfumery) and The Bower of Arachne (the linen shop) written in gold letters above their doors. Burke walked up and down before them, observing everything around him, looking again and again into the same shopwindows and at the crowds moving past, the gentlemen, the vendors, the slaves. He even knelt and examined the street itself, paved in smoothed cobblestones. But after two hours' investigation, Burke had found nothing. Returned to the Calle del Sol, he sat at his desk to think, and when Fernandita brought in his supper he refused the plate of French sausages and rice with a distracted wave of his hand.

"You must ease yourself about hunting that girl," Fernandita said. "Somebody's going to catch her and it might as well be you. We have debts to pay."

"It's not that," Burke said, looking up at her. "I'm quite over that." The usual stoniness returned to Fernandita's face and she left the room, but in a moment she had returned. "I almost forgot," she said. "A boy brought this." She handed Burke a message. It was from Galván, and he'd written only three words: Body not found.

LATER THAT NIGHT, once full darkness had fallen, Burke dressed in trousers and a shirt made of old sailcloth and left his rooms to walk through the city. It was all he could think to do. He hoped that, passing among slaves, visiting their night haunts, he might hear rumors—of Marcita, of the murdered slave, of the others the don mentioned had gone missing. He went to the abandoned lots and shadowy groves where slaves were known to gather for their dances and their guinea magic, but each one he found deserted. The only slave he saw that night he stumbled on by chance—a fresh *bozal* standing outside a tavern, far from any of the slaves' usual places. He seemed agitated; he was staring in through the tavern's window at white men eating and drinking, gnashing his lips.

Burke approached him. "What's the matter?" he asked.

The slave turned to him. Tribal scars ridged his forehead and shoulders. His front teeth were filed into points, and his breath stank of aguardiente. "I lost my little Anto," he said.

Just then the tavernkeeper came out and waved a stained rag at the two of them. "Bah!" he said. "Go on! Get moving!" He snapped the rag at the slave and then at Burke, who, as he leapt back, bumped into a creole passing by. Without breaking stride, the man struck him with his gold-tipped cane, then continued on down the street, paying him no more attention. Burke recognized the fellow—Maroto? Sánchez?—had even shaken his hand at a salon where he'd been invited to play cards and share stories about his cases. He wanted to shout, but by the time he'd overcome his shock at being struck the creole was gone, disappeared into the night. He turned to find the slave with the pointed teeth, but he was gone, too.

After an hour of more wandering, Burke returned to his rooms, lit a lamp, and sat at his desk. The slaves were frightened of something—he could see that in their emptied gathering places and in the eyes of the *bozal*. But what was the connection to Marcita's disappearance? He thought of the head found outside the city, and of the street where Marcita disappeared. He could sense a tie between them, but his brain failed to take hold of it. Outside, the *sereno* called the second hour of morning. Burke took a cigarette from the canister on his desk. Fernandita had just restocked them with the don's money. He struck a match, brought the light to the cigarette tip, then stopped. The labels in Marcita's room—the shop in the Calle O'Reilly with the too-high prices—the cigarette factory next to the field where the slave was found. As each piece clicked into the next the match burned down and singed his fingers.

"Fernandita!" he shouted. "Fernandita!"

After the fourth shout she emerged from her closet, cursing and blinking.

"Go to the captain-general's palace. He'll be up, playing cards. Give him this message." As Burke spoke, he quickly scrawled a letter telling the captain-general he was acting in the affairs of Don Hernán and asking him to send troops to the Pedroso y Compañia factory without delay.

"Why? What's happening?" Fernandita looked about the room, as if someone else might be there.

"I'm not sure yet," Burke said, the unlit cigarette still in his mouth. He shoved the letter in Fernandita's hands. "But I'm going to find out."

At that he left his rooms and ran through the dark streets until he found an idle *volanta* waiting near the cathedral. Dropping a handful of reales into the postilion's palm, Burke yelled for him to drive to the Calle de la Soledad, outside the city. "Race the devil!" he shouted. Then he threw himself into the *volanta*'s seat and the man took off.

THEY WENT PAST THE FIELD where the head had been found, then came to an empty lane just off the paseo—the Calle de la Soledad. The *volanta* pulled to a stop, and Burke got out, telling the driver to wait. The white macadam glowed in the light of the moon, and the air carried the scent of meat cooked over a fire. A night bird called from a far line of trees, but otherwise everything was still. Just up the lane stood the three factories Burke had seen earlier that day when he'd come to inquire about the murder. The snuff mill lay dormant and Burke stepped quickly, carefully past its low, silent hulk. Just beyond it was the yard of the cigarette factory. He halted. The factory's yard was untended, overgrown with weeds and littered here and there with bottles. But light shone through the cracks in its shuttered windows, and, once he stilled his own breathing, Burke could hear the murmur of men talking.

He knew he should wait for the captain-general's soldiers, but he couldn't hold himself back. What were these men up to? Might Marcita still be alive, trapped inside? He crept to one of the windows and edged open a shutter and looked. In the factory's single hall, where women once worked rolling cigarettes, a black-skinned body hung from a hook. It was being stripped by one man while two others worked at one of the old rolling tables, turning a grinder. The grinder jammed just as Burke's gaze fell on it, and one of the men working it kicked at the table while the other shouted. The man stripping the body, cutting meat from the legs, whistled a tune, unbothered. Burke recognized him as the corpulent, red-haired tobacconist from the Gallitos shop.

It took Burke a moment to understand, and once he did he felt his reason trickle away. He couldn't turn—the ghastly sight held him. Instead, without noticing, he leaned forward. His hand was still on the shutter, and it creaked. At that all three men looked up from their work. Burke let go of the shutter. It creaked again, and now they had seen him.

Burke tried to move, tried to run, but a lightness washed forward from the back of his skull. The men at the grinder had snatched knives from the table, and the one stripping the body had picked up an ax. Burke watched, paralyzed. They'd gone, and he could hear the cannibals' footsteps, out of the factory now and on the grass. At last Burke beat back the lightness, pulled his feet from the morass that had gripped them, and ran. Just as he made it to the *volanta,* he heard the trumpets of the captain-general's troops, and two cavalrymen appeared in the street. Burke didn't care to see any more. Bent over in the *volanta's* seat, he heaved, shut his eyes, and ordered the driver to take him home.

"In the sausage!?" Don Hernán repeated, his face green. He was sitting in Burke's bedchamber, slumped in a cane chair. "Oh, my poor cinnamon! To think I—" He stopped. It seemed for the moment he could not bring himself to mention the French sausage again.

Burke lay on his cot. When he'd returned to his rooms he'd felt the lightness return, a sickness overtaking him, and he'd not been able to stand or sit. Now, morning having come, he was explaining his findings to the don, detailing how the three men had roamed the outskirts of the city capturing slaves to butcher. Fernandita stood by the door folding and refolding a cleaned sheet as she listened.

"The shop was a ruse. That's why the price on the cigarettes was so high, to keep people away. Marcita was unlucky. She must have wandered in, looking for new labels for her collection, and that's when they took her."

Outside a bell tinkled, a procession of priests bringing the viaticum to a dying man.

"All of Havana eating slave flesh," the don said. "Horrible!" He

69

sat up, some of the green faded from his face. "But I tell you, I can't understand why. I've thought over the numbers—there couldn't have been much money in it, not nearly as much as the slaves were worth in the field."

The ringing had gone, the priests turned around a corner. What he'd seen through the window of the cigarette factory flashed again before Burke's eyes.

"Don Hernán, who can know the motives of such beasts?"

ONCE THE DON HAD LEFT, Burke called to Fernandita to help him to the window. She held him by the arm, and he pushed aside the curtain and looked out. The sun shone brightly on the harbor ships, ignorant of all that had just passed.

He had been working to save slaves, not trap them, but in the light of the morning his relief had begun to crumble. He'd fashioned excuses, but he'd been willing to hunt Marcita for pay. His mind spun with the thought that he'd become the equal of the men in the factory, that he'd stepped irrevocably away from the goodness he'd once imagined his.

When he turned back from the window, he said to Fernandita, who still held his arm and was smiling uncertainly up at him, "You may tell my next caller that I am taking no more cases."

The smile vanished. "Don't be a fool," Fernandita said. "Not over just the one girl."

But Burke had learned the truth of his position now. Shaking free of Fernandita's hand he stepped back toward his cot. "If the caller insists," he told her, with a glance back toward the masts outside his window, "you may lie and say I am no longer in the city but a lowly crewman at sea." His legs were still weak, and he was exhausted from his night of work, hollowed and brittled by all he'd seen. At the moment he couldn't fathom what he was going to do when his money ran out, but he'd decided his work as a detective in Havana was finished, and in that alone he found solace.

BORDEN'S MEAT BISCUIT

I

Enterprise

In March, during the last weeks before the season of fever returned, all Galveston was filled with talk of conquest. A ship carrying a company of *filibusteros* from the mainland had just sailed for Haiti with plans of empire, and Colonel Timson, a forceful, charismatic fellow who wore a wide-brimmed hat like a planter and swore off all whiskey and cigars, was making the rounds putting together an expedition to topple the government of Honduras and establish a white republic. He had a sharp face reddened by daily shaving, and his tight lips and dark eyes seemed always to be hiding some secret, or perhaps some fury. The man himself was a mystery. I never learned his past, apart from one year he spent as a gin operator in Burwood, Mississippi, nor how he earned his rank, which I came to believe was self-given.

I first caught his attention while passing out handbills for my meat biscuit in the Strand. I spent most mornings in this fashion, stifling my melancholy, awaiting the steamers from Tampico and Veracruz and keeping an eye out for newcomers: I would press the bill into their hands and tell them that a free sample could be obtained at the warehouse. When I stopped Timson in the street, he was attired in a black frock coat faded to gray and worn shiny at the elbows and cuffs. He inspected the bill, then folded it, put it in his coat pocket, and asked if I had a spare hour. He was the first in months to express an interest, so I said I did. We walked about the square and down to the wharves and, without further introduction, he told me of his plans.

"Do you follow Washington?" he asked.

I told him I did not.

"Well, surely men of understanding like yourself know this nation is founded upon the divine harmonies of slave and free. The Northern abolitionists hope to destroy this harmony, and the only way we can stop them is through expanding our institutions." He unrolled each sentence by rote—they were well worn from much use—and every few words he prodded me with his finger. "I have studied the matter closely and determined Honduras as our first acquisition. We will sow her with slaves and petition for statehood. Some may cower at the thought of such an enterprise, but I foresee little resistance to our tropic campaign." Here he took off his hat and drew from inside it a folded sheet of paper, which he opened and showed to me: a newspaper illustration of two *campesinos* dozing next to a burro. "The enemy," he said. He then refolded the picture, taking care to make no new crease, and stuck it again in his hat, which he returned to his head.

"Of course," he continued as we strolled, "there will be a brief period during which I shall preside over a provisional republic, and which my backers will find quite remunerative." Here we paused as several negroes dressed in finery paraded before us, their masters goading them, showing them off to the city's wealthy gathered on the courthouse lawn. Timson leaned closer and whispered. "I have been in contact with agents of President Pierce. They have given me assurances."

We parted, agreeing to meet at some later time. I confess my motives were selfish. I never became a true acolyte of Timson's; I did not believe that the addition of Honduras to our Union, or any amount of new slave states, could head off the reckoning that yet awaits our nation, and to this day every time I hear of a negro lashed or beaten I find myself drawn one inch closer to the abolitionist camp. But Timson could prove the biscuit, I felt, and this I wanted more than anything.

Returning to the Strand, I was accosted by two ruddy-nosed drunks, their mouths curled into devilish grins as they grabbed at my handbills and bellowed, "A sample, Dr. Toad, a sample!" The nickname grew from a rumor about my ingredients, and such treatment was in the normal course of things. But it was not always so. Three years ago the biscuit was birthed into the world with great hope and fanfare. As with all my inventions, my motivation was the alleviation of suffering. To make the biscuit I boiled beef, reducing it from eleven pounds to one, and combined the resulting extract with flour, which I then baked, creating an incorruptible and easily transportable nugget of nourishment. With it, ships at sea would have no worry for starvation, and missionaries and soldiers cut off from supplies would have all the benefit of a full meal in a single bite. Dr. Asa Smith was my partner. He had lodged in my back room for two months when he first arrived in the city, and I had held him in friendship ever since, allowing him to treat cholera patients in my parlor during the occasional epidemic. Though it was his habit to oppose my contrivances, he saw the biscuit's merit and gave over half his small fortune for its support, and together we showed the biscuit at the Great Exhibition in London and sent canisters of it to Arctic explorers and British troops in the Crimea. Everywhere it was met with enthusiastic praise, and on our return to Galveston we manufactured thousands of pounds more.

And then all orders dropped. A committee of army officers in Washington complained of the flavor. Flavor! I made no claims of flavor, only sustenance. Indeed, it is my true belief that a cabal of meat purveyors bribed the committee, for they stood to lose everything to my biscuit. Whatever the cause, it was only the last failure in a long list, ranging from the terraqueous machine to the potato pill and bone bread.

After the committee's report, Dr. Smith and I were left with a warehouse full of meat biscuit, twenty thousand pounds packed in barrels, canisters, and bottles. Often we made our nightly meals upon it—I prepared the biscuit in diverse ways, sometimes in puddings, sometimes in broths, sometimes in pies, sometimes simply toasted. Even so, this was more than Dr. Smith and I could eat on our own were we given until Armageddon.

II

Death's Shadow, from Which Rises the Cooling Safe

It was only in the last season that the fever took my Penelope. I shut myself in the study and turned away from all projects, including the meat biscuit. Overcome by a bleakness of the soul, I spent days tracing the grains of my desk with my fingertips, searching my mind for methods of revivification. I refused food and drink, and after the first night I abandoned hope. I was emptied. She had suffered too many days, and when they took her coffin from the house I could not bear to watch. The sight of her laid out on the bed haunted me so, as did the memory of her constant calling, first for water, then for release. Dr. Smith, who had done his best to ease her pain, managed the affairs of the burial, and I only left the study to follow the black-draped wagon down Avenue P, its horses tired from the many loads forced on them by the fever-ridden island.

Distraught, when I returned from the cemetery I went once more into isolation, plagued by visions of Penelope's deathbed agonies. Yet turning my mind to the rescue of others soon became a salve, and thinking of the fever's coincidence with summer's heat—a fact well known by all but little acted upon—I drew up plans for a sealed box in which men could pass frozen through the pestilential season, untouched by infection. Driven by those deathbed visions, my labors were unceasing, and when I emerged from the study two days later I erected the box in the side yard, near the fig and the oleander we had planted on our wedding day. The box was three feet tall, ten feet long, and six feet wide, piped with ether and built of wooden double walls that I reinforced with iron and lined with a mixture of cotton and corncobs. Completed, it stood like a long dwarf house between the two twiggy nuptial scrubs. For patent purposes, I named it the Cooling Safe. It would be my monument to Penelope's memory. If only I had built the box while she yet lived!

Pleased with the Cooling Safe's construction, I invited Dr. Smith to come inspect it. I waited as he opened the box's door and crawled about inside, tapping the ether pipes and checking my calculations. When he finished, he said nothing, but clasped my hand and looked hard into my eyes before riding back to his office.

The next day I went about the city soliciting volunteers to test the box. The men at the Tremont and on the wharf only shook their heads. They said I had taken "a bad turn." They could not understand. "You shall not freeze me to death, Dr. Toad!" Captain Briggs shouted, twisting his arm from my grip in the Liberty saloon. "Not death!" I countered. "I shall freeze you to life!" But he only chuckled and took his whiskey, as the others had done. I returned home, sullen at their refusal, and as I considered the box our slave boy John tugged at my sleeve and asked about repairing the chicken coop. My mind seized on the opportunity. I gave John some ham and a blanket and put him in the box, showing him the gutta-percha breathing tube and instructing him to knock soundly on the door if he should feel any deleterious effect. At first he was not obliging, but I swore I'd cuff him (an empty threat) and he crawled inside. I shut the door behind him and waited, sitting on the steps of our porch, my chin in my palm, my other hand holding the mourning ring made of Penelope's fine golden hair.

I watched the box for nearly an hour before John banged on the door. I opened it and found him shivering, nearly passed out.

"John, are you all right?" I asked, my arms around his torso as I pulled him free, and he said, teeth chattering, "Yes, master, just a mite cold."

Once I had John clear of the box, I took him into the study, sat him in a chair, and administered a series of tests to his person. His skin was cold to the touch, and I draped a second blanket over his shoulders to stop him shivering.

"Did you feel any spells come upon you?"

"I don't know. It was all dark, and too cold to tell spell from no spell."

I felt his head, his chest, his back, his feet. He had been cooling evenly, moving steadily toward the stasis I had predicted.

"Master," he said to me then. "Please tell me what it is I done to get punished in that shack." He gathered the blankets closer about him and looked up to me. "I promise I won't do it no more."

His mouth was open in pleading, his eyes teary. I held his hand, feeling the tips of his fingers. They had warmed faster than I expected.

III

The Second Meeting with Timson

The day after I met Timson in the Strand, I found him waiting for me outside the warehouse. He was sitting at the door, his head leaned against it, his wide hat low over his eyes. His clothes were dusty and rumpled, and I believe he may have slept in the street. I nudged him awake, and he asked if he might now sample the meat biscuit. He told me he had heard intriguing stories of my career. This I ignored—I knew what others said of me. I toasted him a small portion of the biscuit, and when he bit it, he declared its taste satisfactory. "This manna will feed my army," he said, chewing still as he straightened his coat, "and strengthen its conquering hand." He made a fist and brought it down on an imaginary Honduran's head.

We left the warehouse and walked to the wharves. A steamer was in from Havana, unloading tobacco and bringing news; already the longshoremen were abuzz with talk of a fire that had destroyed much of Matanzas. At the customhouse I fought through a bustling crowd of negroes come to bear away packages for their masters, finally finding the ship's machinist, from whom I collected sheet music. He and I had a compact. In exchange for jars of potato pills (he was one of their rare admirers), he brought me the latest song sheets from a stall in the Calle Obispo. This business completed, Timson and I left the customhouse and moved down the docks until we came to a gap among the cotton bales awaiting the next brig to Liverpool. The bales were stacked into mountains, and boys climbed over them, their laughing voices mixing with the shrieking of gulls and arguing of sailors. We stood in the gap, our backs to the cotton, and watched the busy harbor glinting in the noonday sun. Water lapped against the dock posts beneath us, and Timson pronounced on the divine inspiration of his plans, of God's pact with the white man. "He has provided the African for our labor, and in return we are to raise the African, to bring him religion and feed his body."

"How do you—"

Staring down at me with his fiery eyes, he answered before I could finish, "I am in communication with His Presence."

Eventually I witnessed it. When God spoke to him, Timson would raise his arms to the heavens and one eye would look this way while the other eye looked that.

We left the bales and walked as far as the old pirate camp. Timson talked of Honduras, of her principal products, and of his methods for increasing her productivity—among his favorite was the granting of confiscated haciendas to the second sons of leading Southern families, who would each be required to bring fifteen negro slaves. He asked if I had been married (it was too painful, so I shook my head) and confided in me his love for a clubfooted girl in Burwood, whom he planned to send for once peace was established in his new republic. "When I paid court, she sat on the porch, and only after I had declared myself did she stand before me." Timson rested his foot on a pile of charred brick, the remains of the old camp, and looked out to the gulf, empty and blue, as a breeze struck our faces. "The Lord humbled me with that, but I told her I loved her all the same."

Our conversation ended, we returned to the city, where Timson excused himself, claiming another appointment, and I retreated to the warehouse to look over the song sheets and hum their tunes. Briefly I worried over Timson's scheme, and the general furtherance of bondage, and yet for the biscuit I saw no alternative. Its failure plagued me, and success was worth any price, for men of all color would enjoy the biscuit's benefit. I would back Timson without compunction.

That evening I opened a new canister and made a gravy for Dr. Smith, pouring it over his meat biscuit hash. For myself I fried some biscuit. I like it often this way, simple.

IV

The Cooling Safe Unveiled

I presented the now-tested box to the men of the city. The fever was still ravaging the island. Twenty more had passed away since I had buried Penelope, almost all work had stopped, and the remaining healthy spent their days drifting between street and saloon. They came now, curious, and gathered in the yard. I had John with me to demonstrate, and showed how I had placed him in the box and piped in the ether. Our bodies would be held in stasis, I explained, telling them of John's short experience and ensuing good health. "He spent above an hour in the Cooling Safe," I said, "and returned from it in as fine a fettle as one could hope." Then I proposed the building of a much larger box, big enough to contain the city's entire populace. There, together, we would reside frozen from May until October, waking after the first frost to conduct our commerce in the safe, wintry months. Never again would we suffer from the fever that took my Penelope. The men mocked me, jeered, and threw bottles at the Cooling Safe, and when I asked one, Ashby Hays, a cotton factor, to test the model for himself, he laughed in horror. "You'd ask me, a white man, to step in that nigger box?"

He led the rest away in a grumbling mob, back toward the pestilential city, and I stood in the yard with John, head hung in defeat, bruised where a bottle had struck me on the shoulder, and felt—it was a low moment—that I would not care if the fever took them all.

V

On Baptism

Does one baptism wash away another? I hope not, for I remember when Penelope and I were baptized together before the congregation by Reverend Hall, and if men can claim but one baptism, that is the one I will claim. Afterward, the both of us wet and clean in our white baptismal garments, we sat together in the sun and she smiled and touched my hair as I held her hand, running my fingers over her bare wrist.

But Timson was keen to baptize me himself, and not wanting to lose favor I walked with him to the gulf, where he took me into the waters, asked me to confess my faith in Jesus and His bond with the white man, and then dropped me under just as a wave approached, the sea foam rushing over his back and my pliant body. He pulled me up again and said, "Praise God!" and the men from his company, watching from the shore, let out a cheer.

It had been several weeks since I had first met him, and support for the expedition was mounting. Timson was dining in some of the city's finest homes and lodged now on the third floor of the Tremont. We walked along the beach as our clothing dried, the sun shining down a clear curtain of light, and Timson told me that in a chest he kept plans for his new capital city. He said the streets would be modeled on those of old Jerusalem, and that already he had families from as far away as Boston sending him deposits for plots of land.

"We'll use palm tree bark to pave the roads," he said, "and leaves for fans." He put some shredded bark in my hand, pressing it to reveal its springiness, then slapped my shoulder and left me in the Strand.

When I met Dr. Smith at the warehouse for dinner, I showed him the bark. He sniffed it, then set it on the table, considering it for some time. "I pray this will not prove another disappointment," he said, his eyes sorrowful and heavy, his face softened with doubt. He had too much tact to go further. We rarely talked about the past, and never about the Cooling Safe.

"It won't," I promised.

That night we ate the biscuit dry, straight from the canister.

VI

A New Scheme Brings About Protest

I decided John and I would use the box. Together we would pass safely through the remaining months of fever, isolated and frozen, and show the city the efficacy of the Cooling Safe. But once my plan became known, I was troubled with complaints from the public. "For a day I would allow a white man and a negro to share common chambers," Judge Carter said, standing with two aldermen on the porch, "but for perhaps the entire summer?"

In answer I promised to install a curtain, creating a whites' side and a negroes' side. "But do not fret, John," I assured the boy once the deputation had left. "You and I both shall survive the fever's cruel menace."

He looked at me, silent, his arms ashy from cleaning the fireplace.

"And just think," I added. "If my estimates are correct, with annual freezing we shall live two hundred years!"

VII

The Deal Is Struck

I did not see Timson for three weeks. He went about the city in a velvet-trimmed suit and had most of his backers lined up and his company of men filled. But we had yet to draft an agreement. I despaired. Had he found a replacement for the biscuit? I neglected the handbills and spent my days in the warehouse, waiting.

Fortunately, my uncertainty was not prolonged. At the month's end Timson moved his lodgings from the Tremont to his steamer, the *Maria*—payment for its use was being footed by twelve Houston bankers—and sent a messenger to request that I join him. It was night, and I had dined already with Dr. Smith, so I took my coat, locked the warehouse, and followed the messenger, a skinny lad of thirteen, down to the ship. There Timson introduced me to Lyons and Wayhurst, two Louisiana planters who were to provide the expedition with guns. We went aboard and toured the deck, Timson guiding us with a lantern past the paddle wheel and the stack. The harbor was black all around us, here and there lights from boats and dock houses meeting us from across the empti-ness like phantom eyes, and the only sound was the chug of the night steamboat returning from the mainland. In the captain's quarters we sat while Timson led us in prayer, raising his right hand high as he called down Jehovah and beseeched Him to dwell in the cabin. Lyons and Wayhurst exchanged worried looks, but I motioned for them to have no fear, this was all in the normal course of things. Timson stamped his foot, his eyes drifted, and he spoke as if through his nose, hissing his words. "Praise ye! Praise ye! I bless this transaction!" Then he let his hand fall and banged it on the table. "We have an agreement," he said to the two planters, his voice calm, the red retreating from his face, his eyes settling into their regular tracks.

The cabin was now very still, none of us knowing what to do next, and we waited in the quiet until Lyons or Wayhurst—I can't remember which—said, "Excellent!" The silence broken, they arranged for the guns' delivery, shook hands all around, then went into town seeking whores. I watched them through the porthole, their arms at each other's backs as they walked up the dock toward the lights of the city. I exhaled, clearing my mind of envy (in my great loneliness I too have been tempted), and looked over at Timson. He had not noticed the planters' departure; he was busy signing Honduran banknotes for the payment of his men. They were for a hundred reales each, and had been printed four to a sheet.

"Do you still desire the biscuit?" I asked, watching as Timson cut the notes with great care. I saw before me sailors starving at the antipodes, children in need of precious nutriment. Must they suffer due to the whim of a fickle public? "Please tell me the meat purveyors have not gotten to you with their slanders."

The *Maria* rocked and creaked ever so slightly in the harbor waters. Timson looked up from the notes. "The Lord spoke to me of the biscuit," he said, and I hung on his words—so much hung on them! "He said I should feed my men by your bread and none other."

I rejoiced, shook Timson's hand, and bowed several times, not caring if he thought me a madman. Ready to complete the business, we went over the final agreement. Dr. Smith and I would provide Timson's militia with the remaining meat biscuit, supplying the entire expedition, and in return we asked only two things. I requested that Timson write a testimonial to the biscuit's goodness, and Dr. Smith wanted a banana plantation. Timson offered no objection, we both signed the contract, and it was done.

VIII

The Altar of Discovery

With my new plan for the box I was exuberant, despite the mocking of the city men. I instructed John to roll up the carpets and prepare the house for our long absence, and hired a reliable man,

Hiram Wheelock, to open the Cooling Safe after the first frost, paying him five dollars in gold and promising him five more once he greeted us at the heat's end. I also retained James Johnson, the cartwright, to do the services in the case of Hiram's passing, and contracted with Levy the merchant to supply the ether. Twice a week he would deliver a new jug and note for me any variations shown by the gauges. The city was silent, every corner hung with death, and as I went about making my arrangements, I ran into Dr. Smith, with whom I had not spoken since the day I had first shown him the box. He took me aside and asked in hushed tones if I truly meant to go through with the freezing. When I said yes, he shook his head. "I have remained silent too long. Every man mourns in his own way, but this must stop!" I ignored his remonstrance, and he suggested I at least try a pig first. "Hog flesh is sound for experiment," he said, but I slipped from his grasp and told him I needed no counsel.

Yet I did fear, briefly, that during our entombment the fever's toll would mount higher than in seasons past, would take the whole city and leave no one to wake us, or that perhaps another hurricane would cross the island and wash the city along with the box into the bay. Still, enterprise requires risks. The death of one inventor and one slave boy was a small offering to lay at the altar of discovery, should such a misfortune occur.

IX

A Ceremonious Departure

The day Timson sailed for Honduras, I went down to the docks like everyone else. He had filled the steamer's stores to the fullest with meat biscuit, leaving room only for the guns and his robes of state, fashioned from the old curtains of the Star Theater. A brass band played, people cheered, and Timson's men lined up on the steamer and waved their hats over their heads in farewell.

The crowd pressed close as girls handed flowers up to the men, and after some minutes, in answer to cries from his admirers, Timson came to the railing and addressed us. "With this endeavor," he said, shouting so all could hear, "we shall not only preserve our Union, we shall perform God's work on this earth, fulfilling His holy plans for slave and free!"

We applauded, and several in the crowd shot off their guns in celebration as the steamer broke away from the wharf. Timson moved to the stern and raised his hands, and between the blasts of the ship's horn, over the churn of the engine, we could hear him blessing our city. Everyone stayed, watching until the steamer had cleared the harbor and rounded the tip of the island. Then we let out another cheer and some, mostly children, ran across the island's humped middle to the gulf, to watch the steamer pass into the broad waters. Soon she was beyond the horizon and all that could be seen was the last puff of smoke belched from her stack, grayish black on the gulf's far edge, and then this too disappeared. I returned to the warehouse. Dr. Smith was already there, standing beside the table and looking out the window, his hands clasped behind his back. "Today I treated a man for the fever," he said. "First of the season." I turned my eyes to the floor, grimy near the stove, and said nothing. That night I fried us some of the biscuit— even after Timson's men had taken all they could, we were left with above a thousand pounds.

X

In Which Dr. Smith Plays the Hero

The morning I had set for our confinement, I woke to find John gone. I called his name throughout the house and in every corner of the yard and heard only the echo of my own voice. I wondered if he had been stolen—in the midst of the fever there had been a rash of slave thefts, the stolen negroes turning up in the market at New Orleans—and then if he had run away. I had no time to investigate and, hoping the latter was the case, wished him good journey and readied myself for the box. I slipped the ring of Penelope's hair over my finger, kissed it, and stepped into the yard. Dressed in a wool garment of my own design, I performed a series of exercises, bending at the waist and stretching my arms, then crouching and holding my hands at my hips, in order to even the blood for optimal freezing. I had not seen a soul all morning, yet as I was opening the box's iron door, Dr. Smith came riding up. I hailed him, but he did not answer. Instead he leapt from his horse, bolted toward me, and gave me two hard punches in the jaw. The second one felled me.

"You goddamn fool," he said when I woke. "Do you mean to kill yourself?"

I scrabbled toward the safe, but he held me down, and only then, as I spent myself in struggle against him, did I begin to see my madness. The suffering—I so wished to end the suffering!

XI

Despair

I spent the next weeks walking the island and dining with Dr. Smith, who had developed the habit of reading aloud from pamphlets on banana cultivation while at table. During the mornings I drafted letters trumpeting the biscuit's success and our plans for renewed production, which I would post to various government agencies and newspapers of record once I had word from Honduras. Each day, awaiting this word, I twisted in currents of emotion, from hope to dread and back again, my only solace wandering the dunes and feeling the gulf breeze whip over me. At times I thought of slave ships putting in at Trujillo, to supply Timson's new plantations. My heart fell at the vision, but was swiftly buoyed by another: the biscuit proved before the world.

Then, a month after his leaving to the fanfare of the city, we got news of Timson's campaign. His men returned in rags, arriving in twos and threes on the ships of charitable captains, and told their stories in the saloons and on the docks. The Honduran army had made quick work of them, and after only a few days of jungle fighting Timson had been captured and hanged in the plaza at Comayagua. I caught one man on the wharf. He had a bandage on his head and would not answer any question, any hello or how are you. I followed him as he walked down to the water and along the beach, poking at the jetsam left by the last tide. Finally I clutched his arm.

"The biscuit?" I asked. "The biscuit?"

He fixed me with his good eye, sunken and glassy. "One half dumped in the bay," he said, "the other half left in the jungle."

I fell to my knees. It was the final blow.

XII

Leave-taking

After I met Timson's man, I drifted in a stupor for a week, passing from the city to the wastes and back again. The clouds came in low over the gulf, the rain fell gray and cold, and by the time the sun returned, I knew I could live here no longer, where every effort proved another folly. These streets, these shores offered no succor for the loss of my Penelope, only frustrations to inspire the laughter of my neighbors.

"I am sure," Dr. Smith said, smiling and raising his glass, "that in Manhattan you will find an environment as nourishing to your creative faculties as the biscuit has been to your corporeal ones." This was during our last dinner together, on the eve of my departure. Dr. Smith had taken the news of Timson hard, but charged me with no fault. Already he was full of plans for turning the warehouse into a medical college, where he would meet daily with his students to pick over fresh corpses.

"I hope you are right," I answered, accepting his toast and his present of a meal of fresh beef. Yet I was unable to enjoy either. The Honduran debacle had left me in a poor state. My soul, abandoned once more to the arid climes of despair and disappointment, had dried and cracked within me, so that it rattled in the hollows of my body like chips of bone. And lately the abolitionist press had begun to mock me. They called me mercenary for my attachment to Timson's campaign, raising too my experiments with the Cooling Safe. But then I roused myself. Even in my depths I could glimpse the world we were making; it shone like a jewel in the sun.

The next morning, the morning I left Galveston, I dropped the remaining stock of meat biscuit in the water. The canisters broke upon the jetty rocks, and gulls fought over the crumbs afloat on the waves. I stood there, watching for nearly an hour before turning my back on what I was determined would be my last failure.

THE TRAITOR OF ZION

THEY HAD BECOME SOMETHING of a fascination of mine: communes cut out of the interior, new societies where all were equal and either Jesus or Liberty reigned. Some days, after reading an account of a blind prophetess leading her followers to Illinois, or of a mill town where all shared labor and wealth equally, I yearned to give up my life and join them. I felt as if we lived in a hurtling age. It seemed all humanity stood on a precipice, that in the distance, beyond the coal smoke and the tangle of telegraph wires, could be spied a shining metropolis where men would be re-formed. But I spent my days stuck in my father's shop—at twenty-three I was his peer in making the fiddles and other cheap instruments we sold to travelers embarking from the docks—and my nights in drink with friends. I need only walk the streets of my Baltimore, pass a slave carrying bricks on his crooked back or a rheumy-eyed sailor, ruined by the sea, begging alms and ale, to feel the rottenness in my soul. Men could not be changed, and I, one among millions, would never make it to any dream city.

Even so, the yearning never left me. One night, during yet another of my regular debauches, I rose without a word and left my friends in a steaming oyster house. I had seen notices in the paper of a Hebronite meeting. Their leader and revelator, Josiah Kershaw, was touring the East to summon new followers to the city he was raising on Peaine Island, a wilderness in the far northern reaches of Lake Michigan. All week the papers had mocked Kershaw. To them he was a gross fabricator, the great paradise he promised a myth, the prophecies on which he claimed his authority pure forgeries. But I was intrigued. His talk of harmony, of plain lives lived according to rule, stirred my hopes. I had passed the last weeks in a violent melancholy, pining for a woman who didn't know me, a ship captain's young wife. Increasingly I had seen my future, bound by an invisible chain to the worktable just like my father. And so, unsteady on my feet after five whiskeys, I searched for the inn where the meeting was to be held. By the time I found it my heart beat heavily in my chest and sweat dripped from my skin. My nerves were electric with anticipation.

Eyes turned to look at me when I stumbled into the room. The meeting was already under way. At the front a graybeard clutched a Bible and kept his eyes shut as he recited a prayer. I sat in the back and gripped my knees to keep from swaying. The graybeard droned on. People yawned and scratched their noses. After fifteen more minutes of this—the prayer was unending!—I could barely master myself. I was an imbecile. There was nothing for me here. I glanced at the door, but before I could rouse the courage to get back up, the graybeard sat and another man stood.

"Those who walk in the way of the Lord will receive His blessings," he shouted, and with those words and that marshal's voice I was seized. My drunkenness lifted from me. My eyes steadied, my mind ceased to yaw, my limbs stiffened with sober life. I recognized Kershaw from the newspaper illustrations. He was tall and spare, with a trimmed auburn beard and a high forehead seemingly shaped for the guarding of truths. His eyes glittered as if catching the wonders of his heavenly Guide. He paced before us, and something in him called to me. Without knowing why, I hungered for his blessing.

Five years earlier, he told us, he had been a coal shoveler in Chautauqua County. There, one black night, angels of the Lord bearing heavenly candles had shown themselves to him and revealed a golden scroll hidden in a cave. On this scroll he found descriptions of Peaine Island. The Lord had chosen it as the site for a holy city, a place where men would live in harmony under new laws and seek pleasure in labor, purity in distance from all the corruptions of the East. Already the city was begun. Kershaw had registered it as Port Hebron, after the ancient city of refuge, but when it reached its ordained population of 144,000 it would take its true name of Zion. Then ambassadors from all the world's nations would wait upon him and his followers, Kershaw told us, and Jesus would descend to take His golden throne. I felt the island rise inside me: the pines, the clear water, the small bay, the city shining like a diadem in the lake. The Lord was speaking.

The next morning, as I departed, my father damned me for a fool. He stood as I packed my set of Italian tools and forms and enough cured maple and ebony for a dozen violins. At last he called me cruel for abandoning him and refused to give me his hand in farewell. Ever since my mother died I had been his sole companion, though it had been a companionship passed in silence. His words pained me—I had always been a dutiful son, always done as he asked—but I had heard the call.

I TRAVELED BY RAIL TO BUFFALO and there waited a week for the steamer that took me up the lakes. I spent my days onboard watching the shore, which grew wilder once we left Lake Erie and passed Detroit. The stands of birch and pine along Huron seemed unending. Isolated wisps of smoke, from a cabin or a camp of loggers, signaled the only life.

When at last we put in at the Mackinac settlement, surely one of the remotest in our Union, the sailors shoved their way into the pine-board bars that lined the harbor beneath the fort. Such places repulsed me now, and I and my fellow Hebronites—we'd soon found each other on the ship—walked along the beach and talked of our new lives on Peaine Island. It was on this walk that I saw my first whiskey trader. He sat on a shop porch, wrapped in furs. His cheeks were dirt-stained, his eyes as smoldering coals. He watched me and the other Hebronites as we strolled past, and his look made me shiver. Soon I would learn of the hatred the traders felt for us, but as yet I was ignorant. I tried to shake the look from me as I walked to the boat. The next morning the steamer left Mackinac, passed through the Straits, and called a little past noon at Port Hebron.

It was late September. Already a thousand Hebronites had settled the island, and the chosen city was a trim cluster of cabins and cottages spread along the back of the bay. Directly after we stepped onto the dock we were taken to the Temple and brought one by one before the Council of Elders. To them we professed our faith in the Lord and His Revelator, Josiah Kershaw. Our covenant recorded, the elders gave us our tasks. There was no demand for instruments, so I was sent to a stout, red-cheeked cooper named Pickle. I was his only worker. He gave me a corner of his cabin for my quarters and allowed me to hang my violin in the window, in the small hope of attracting customers for my own trade. My first night on the island he told me his story. A widower, he'd left five grown children behind after hearing Josiah's call in Toledo. He'd been taking part in a Presbyterian synod on hymnals, he said, and had never before thought to stray from his church until, stuck in a crowd on the courthouse lawn, he listened to Josiah tell of a perfect city in the lakes where the Lord spoke and men lived as one.

OVER THE NEXT WEEKS I found Peaine Island just as I had hoped. Our lives were ordered, all were cared for, and each day had its purpose. Sabbaths were set aside for Temple services and rest. After worship I would play my violin or walk into the island's deep wood. Seventh days, to which all men were subject, were given to the building of the kingdom: mine often found me engaged in road clearing, preparing boulevards for the throngs of newcomers Josiah prophesied. And the other five days were given to our own labor. Within a week Pickle had me trained in all the minor points of splitting and planing barrel staves. In the mornings I rose to work, rested only for lunch, and in the evenings I sat at Pickle's table, listening as he read from the Bible and *The Book of Truths*—the volume, printed by Josiah, that contained his first revelations and the rules by which we lived. By the light of a single candle we took our supper, corncakes and molasses with the occasional helping of bacon or ham.

The only break in our routine came when we made sorties against the whiskey traders. Every capable man on the island drilled with the militia on two of his seventh days, and we drew lots to decide who would be called on each week in the event of a sortie. I had learned about the whiskey traders soon after my arrival. They had lived on the island before Josiah and the first Hebronites came to take possession, and had kept a store by the bay, sold whiskey to the Indians in breach of the law, and idled away their days in corruption and filth. Josiah drove them out. Their souls were broken, he said. They were nothing more than the tarred stains of what we had left behind, ungoverned men who shut their eyes to the light of the Lord. Now they lived in nomad camps on the islands that surrounded our own, moving between those and the Manitous to the south or Mackinac and the Charlevoix coast to the east. Josiah had consecrated what was once theirs; he had cleansed their cabins and trapping grounds of their sin and given their land and possessions to his first followers to serve the Lord's purpose. Ever since, the whiskey traders, in their blindness, burned for vengeance. Some nights they came across the lake to steal chickens or a pig, and some nights we sought them out in their camps and put an ax through their whiskey barrels. In this way an uneasy peace was kept.

Under Pickle's roof I earned a simple happiness through daily toil and praisegiving. Winter came swiftly. Deep snows covered the island, ice locked the lake. Finally the spring. I had found what I had sought and eagerly looked forward to the Day of the 144,000. Then, Josiah told us, all people would be judged and the world would be shaped anew. I trembled at the thought—I prayed for my father and my former companions, that they might be prepared. But I awaited the day with fervor.

So might my life have continued, so might that day have come, had I never known Dorothea.

PICKLE'S WORK YARD FRONTED ON JOSIAH STREET, offering a view of the shops along the harbor, and it was there I first saw her. I was leaned against my ax in rest, and she was stopped in the street to gather up the lengths of patterned fabric that had come loose from her bundle. When she glanced back, her eyes caught mine. That was enough.

This, of course, could not really have been the first time I had seen Dorothea Bainbridge. She came to town once a week with her mother, and so must have walked past me before. No doubt my eyes had chanced upon her in the Temple as well. But only with that met glance did she wake my slumbering heart. I felt a fool. How had I not recognized her earlier, how had I not understood sooner that she was to be the sole repository of my love? To make up for my belated revelation I embarked on a careful study of her person whenever she passed. I discovered that her cheeks dimpled when she smiled, that she most often wore her hair in two looping braids, that she wrote poems about fairies and angels (this when I picked up a scrap of paper she'd left in her pew in the Temple). I suffered when she giggled—wishing I was the one making her laugh—and delighted when she frowned, imagining myself her comforter.

I burned with the very thought of her.

My various secret pinings in Baltimore were nothing to this. I was plunged in turmoil, so much so that Pickle worried for my soul and offered to redouble his prayers. Occasionally Dorothea glanced at me, but always I was too shy to introduce myself. Then, in late spring, as I was leaning once again on my ax and watching her walk past the work yard on her way to Teague's store, a breeze came up the bay and whisked her bonnet off her head. I ran to it and snatched the bonnet before it could land in a pile of night soil. "William Ames, violin maker," I said, and, bowing, presented the bonnet to her. I pointed back toward the window in Pickle's cabin: "My shop." I did not add that it occupied only a corner of the cabin, and that this corner also served as my home.

Dorothea settled the bonnet on her head and tucked in first one raven braid, then the other. With each movement she made I ached.

"I'm here every day, and I'd be glad to play for you," I said.

She gave no answer, and I was about to let her walk away when I thought again of what Josiah had said the night of my conversion, that the blessed were those who seized the gifts the Lord put before them.

"May I call on you?" I said, forcing out the words.

She had already gone a few steps, but at that she stopped. "I thank you for my bonnet, Mr. Ames, but my father doesn't allow callers."

"I'll plead with him," I said.

"That wouldn't be any use."

"I'll wait by your farm, then. I can walk you to town or to the Temple. If you don't want me, just send me off." At this her face colored. I had gone too far. "I apologize," I said. "I did not mean—"

"Come next Wednesday," she said quickly, her voice pitched at a whisper: her mother had emerged from Teague's and was calling her. "I make no promises. My father might not let you in." Then she ran to her mother, and the two of them walked up the street until they disappeared around the other side of the bathhouse.

I COULD NOT BELIEVE MY FORTUNE. I had been bold, and the Lord had blessed me. On the agreed-upon Wednesday I left Pickle's work yard an hour early and walked to the Bainbridge farm.

Since my meeting with Dorothea I had spent my spare moments carving hands. With the clearest blocks of scrap pine I could find, I sat by my lamp each evening and whittled. I planned to present the best of the lot to Dorothea and had worked out what I would say. "Might I exchange this rude carving, which I have gripped so delicately all week, for its truer, purer model?" The sixth hand came as near to perfect as I could get. I clutched it by its fingers now as I walked, warming it with my flesh.

The Bainbridge farm lay in the remoter, southern quarter of the island, beyond the village of New Nazareth. I found the cabin at the end of a track that led first through a birch wood and then into a clearing planted with potatoes. As I walked I had assured myself of victory, but now that I approached the Bainbridge cabin I grew nervous. What if Dorothea's father refused me? I considered methods for clandestine courtship. Secret meetings, a hollowed tree for depositing notes.

These imaginings proved unnecessary: though he received me coldly, Bainbridge let me in.

"Mr. Ames," he said upon opening the door. He led me to the cabin's crude parlor, where Dorothea sat working on a stocking. A paperboard screen and blankets slung over strings were all that divided the cabin into rooms. On the walls hung a few newspaper illustrations of Mexican scenes, from the recent war. A glass hutch filled with dull china stood across from the door, and the rest of the furniture took the form of trunks, save for the chairs gathered around the hearth. I was offered the one next to Dorothea while Bainbridge sat across from us, beside his wife. Dorothea glanced up, then returned to her stocking, and Bainbridge stared at the two of us while his wife poked at the fire. Every attempt I made at a pleasantry—on the weather, on the last Sabbath's sermon—was met with a "hmph" by Bainbridge and silence by Dorothea and her mother.

This continued for some time, and I despaired. Was my love to founder so quickly? Then Bainbridge rose to visit the privy, and, at a nod from her mother, Dorothea spoke. "I'm glad you came," she said, putting down the stocking and grinning up at me. "I was worried you wouldn't."

"I had to." With that I offered her the wooden hand and made my speech. Her cheeks reddened, and she took the hand and gave me hers in return. Dorothea's mother had focused her eyes on the small fire and was pretending to ignore us. I wondered then if she had argued for me. For a full five minutes I clutched Dorothea's hand. She pulled it away only when the scrape of the back door announced her father's return.

Once a week, all through the rest of May and into June, I called on Dorothea. Each of my visits followed the same pattern. We would sit in silence as her father watched us, me with my hands folded, Dorothea working on a stocking. Then, once Bainbridge absented himself, her mother would turn away, pretending to contemplate some particular coal, and I would present my gift—another hand, so that I might hold both, and after that a piece of polished burl I called her cheek, which I gave Dorothea in exchange for a kiss of its original. In those rare free minutes we would talk of our days or play teasing games with one another. Once she read me a poem, and another time she made me keep silent while she searched my face. The moment I left her I ached as if fevered, and with each visit it seemed our souls were being knit together.

At our sixth meeting, though, I found her altered.

As before, she worked on a stocking while her father sat with us, but when he left, rather than wake into the girl I had come to know, she stared into her lap. Her mother, sitting across from us as always, ignored the fire and twisted a handkerchief in her fingers.

"Dory," I said. But she didn't look up. "Dory, what is it?"

Then came the scraping of the back door—her father returning sooner than usual. In a moment he was standing over me and telling me it was time to leave.

"I hope you got to say your good-byes," he said once we were outside. "That's the last of your calls, Mr. Ames."

"I don't understand," I said. "My intentions are honorable." I wondered if this was what concerned him. "I hope to marry Dorothea."

"I won't permit it," he said.

His flat refusal surprised me. I stood there more flabbergasted than hurt.

"Sir," I said, "there must be something I can do."

"Nothing," he said.

"But, Mr. Bainbridge," I protested, "surely—"

"You'll get my permission the day you're raised to the Order!" he shouted, and his face grew fiery. He meant to say I had no hope. The Order of Maccabaeus was the highest honor ordained by Josiah. It had as yet no members. I could not understand Bainbridge's stubbornness, and to distract my sick heart—for with each passing moment hurt pumped in—I spent my long walk home cursing him and his arrogance.

IT WAS SOME WEEKS AFTER that last meeting with Dorothea— lost weeks, despairing weeks—that Josiah summoned everyone to the Temple. For four days he had kept himself shut in the Chamber of the Most Holy. While I had been courting Dorothea doubts had been spreading across the island. According to *The Book of Truths,* with the passing of spring we were to have left the Years of Preparation and entered the Years of Manifestation. By now thousands were supposed to be arriving each week. Instead there had been only a trickle of new converts. And where were the promised wonders, the signs of the New Age? Why hadn't angels appeared on Mount Nebo, or fire broken the sky to devour the homes and stores of those sliding into apostasy? Some were saying our faith had fallen short, that we need only trust more in the Lord. Others whispered that Josiah and the elders were in secret taking new wives, like the Mormons of Utah, and the Lord was displeased. Still others, couching their words in the claim that they were merely repeating what they'd heard, accused Josiah of fooling us all with humbuggery. The doubts could no longer be ignored, and at the most recent Sabbath Josiah had announced he was going into the Chamber of the Most Holy to beseech the Lord to show him where we had erred. Each day I had prayed for him. My faith had never wavered.

As I entered the Temple that day, my eyes sought Dorothea and soon found her raven braids peeking from beneath her bonnet. She sat with her father and mother near the front. In the last weeks I had felt as if part of me had sickened and died. There was little more than a cool emptiness left within my chest. Pickle had been solicitous, warning me of destruction and praying I'd return to reason and moderation. Now if I saw Dorothea it was only from a distance, here in the Temple or when she came to town with her mother to Teague's store or with her father during his visits to Josiah. It was rumored Bainbridge was being considered for eldership. Always she would bow her head rather than meet my eyes. I still had not learned the reason for the breaking of our courtship, and the letter I had left for her at Teague's went unanswered. I tried to keep from looking at her, to stare at the rafters or out the windows, but it was impossible. With her back to me I could study her without consequence: her shawl-wrapped shoulders, her bare neck, her bonneted head. Was she happy?

Once everyone was settled, Josiah stepped through the door at the front of the sanctuary, bowed his head as he walked through the Arch of the Blood, and mounted the pulpit. He looked out over us, and an even deeper quiet fell upon the pews.

"There has been confusion and uncertainty," he began, his voice calm. "I've shared it myself. We have come to the site of Zion, we have begun building the city, and yet we look around us and wonder, Where are the multitudes? Last night, the fourth night of my vigil, the Lord put me into a deep sleep, then took me up and showed me a vision of our island. I saw Port Hebron, I saw the forest and the farms, I saw the lake around us, wide as a sea." Now his voice began to rise. His hands gripped the pulpit's sides. His eyes flashed. "The Lord made me to look at the lake and, lo, fire appeared on the horizon, blazing toward our shores. The Lord said, 'This unholy fire you must quench.' Then the fire fell away, and in the middle of the island a pit opened and out of the pit came a cloud of pestilence. The Lord showed me the pestilence spreading among us. It killed everybody it touched. The Lord's voice said, 'This unholy plague you must cure.' I said to the Lord, 'The fire I understand, the traders who circle our island. But the plague? The plague I do not understand.'"

Josiah gazed at the assembly room's ceiling and stretched out his arms, as if still in dialogue with the heavens. "'There is a sickness among you,' He said. 'I will not send My Son to reign over the impure.' 'But what is this sickness, and how am I to cure it?' I asked. 'You will not see it, you will not know it, you will not cure it, but I will send a Judge who will do these things,' He said. 'You must make ready for him. You must build him a house, a seat from which he can spy out your pestilence.' The Lord then showed me how we are to build this house, and I have spent all morning setting down His instructions here." Josiah waved a paper scribbled with notes. "We begin work tomorrow. Praise be to the Lord."

Hunched over the pulpit, sweating, exhausted, he awaited our response. The room remained silent. Perhaps the doubters were considering whether the vision quelled their anxieties, the accusers of humbuggery assessing its authenticity. But after only a few seconds we answered in unison, each of us shouting the words Josiah had taught us: "Glory and thanks to the Lord for His guiding hand!"

A few nights later I was in my corner of Pickle's cabin, playing my violin, when Elder Williamson came to the door. It was past ten—darkness had finally fallen—and Pickle was readying himself for sleep. Elder Williamson told me to get my rifle. Some whiskey traders had come from Mackinac and set fire to Elder Hunt's cabin. They'd not yet been so bold, and even though the cabin was saved Josiah had ordered a sortie to chase them; since the vision he'd demanded more vigilance. After Elder Williamson left I splashed my face with water. My previous weeks on sortie duty had been quiet and I felt unprepared. Bidding Pickle good night, I took my rifle and went to the dock. The others had already begun the prayer. Josiah was there, placing his hand on each one's forehead. I raced up and he put his hand to mine.

We paired into canoes; I was matched with a man named Spofford. I didn't know him well. He'd arrived at the island after me and worked in one of the logging camps. Josiah had elected to lead us himself, and at his orders we paddled out of the bay toward the near islands to the east, the likeliest place we'd find the whiskey traders. Above us a thick spangle of stars cast a faint light on the water. As Josiah had instructed, we took care with our paddles, guarding against every needless splash.

Halfway to Garden Island we spied a rocking lantern. I had heard stories of ghosts on the lake, and I started, but Spofford reached a hand back to quiet me, then, following Josiah, steered us toward the light. As we drew nearer, I saw it was only an Indian in his canoe, night fishing. Josiah gave him a present of smoked beef and a small sack of cornmeal, and the Indian told us that he'd seen the whiskey traders pass three hours earlier, heading toward the notch bay on Garden Island's western point. We paddled in that direction and soon made out the glimmer of the traders' fire on the shore, heard their shouts echo across the lake.

"I'd say they're a few sheets," Spofford whispered back to me. We went past the notch, to a narrow spit of land just to the east, and pulled our canoes up the beach. Once we were in the wood, Josiah gave his instructions. Elder Williamson would lead four men through the trees to a position behind the whiskey traders' camp while the others crept along the sands. We were only to give the traders a scare, Josiah warned us, but enough of a scare to show them we were prepared to fight. After Elder Williamson's party took a five-minute start, the rest of us set out along the shore with Josiah.

The traders had bivouacked at the tree line, their camp not fifty feet from the water, and as we took our positions along the lake's edge I counted them. There were six circled around the fire, and they passed a jug while one among them, a blond-bearded man wrapped in furs and skins, bellowed a story about killing a bear. They didn't see us. The fire was too bright in their eyes, their attentions too occupied by the story.

I looked to Josiah, who was holding up his hand. He dropped it and let out an animal screech. At that Spofford raced off to set fire to the traders' canoes and the rest of us shot our rifles into the air and hooted like crazed owls. From the darkness of the wood Williamson and his men echoed us.

The whiskey traders leapt up at the tumult. They reeled and stumbled drunkenly as they looked about in terror.

"Who's there?" one of them called, aiming his rifle at one blackness after another.

"Damned God-squawkers!" another shouted as he sat back down and applied himself to the jug.

"We didn't mean for it to burn," pleaded a third, and knelt in the sand.

We stood in our places and kept up our hooting. Behind us the lake, black and calm, lapped at the shore. Down the beach the traders' canoes were in full blaze.

We were about to return to our own canoes when the trader who'd been telling the story bolted toward us with a shout of "Goddamn it!" We were not prepared for such a turn, and nobody moved to stop him. By luck he came right at Josiah and tackled him. "Got one of you now!" the trader shouted. Josiah lay struggling on the sand, pinned beneath the trader's knees. Something glittered in the starlight. A knife. My stomach lurched. Without thinking I rushed at the trader and swung the butt of my rifle into his temple. I pushed him off and gave my hand to Josiah, who took it, rose, and whistled for the sortie's end. The remaining whiskey traders fled into the trees with their gear. Only after the last had gone did I return to Josiah's attacker. I shook the man, but he didn't stir. I felt him. Already his body was cooling.

As the others circled Josiah, I stayed beside the trader's body. His face revealed that he was my own age. On his chest lay a necklace of animal teeth, among which was a silver locket. I opened it and a loop of fiery hair fell onto my palm. Bound in its tight circlet, it had the feel of some new metal. I imagined a faraway sitting room, then a darkly lit brothel of the sort I and my companions in Baltimore had always been too timid to enter. What woman had been in possession of the trader's heart? My own clenched quickly with the thought of Dorothea. I replaced the hair and snapped the locket shut. Blood now seeped from the side of the trader's head and had begun to soak the sand.

I was overcome. I thought of the trader's family, of the red-haired woman, and imagined all the better ways I could have stopped him, the ways I could have saved Josiah without killing. I was a sinner, a brute.

Meanwhile, as I watched over the trader's body, the others talked. As of yet there had been no bloodshed between us and the whiskey traders. If anyone learned of what had happened, Josiah warned, there would be more killing. Elder Williamson asked what should be done, and Josiah related his plan. The other traders had only seen their fellow disappear onto the beach and could be certain of nothing. We would take the body to the canoes and dispose of it in the lake. The true account of the night could never be disclosed: when asked, we would say the trader who had attacked Josiah fled into the wood, after his fellows. Once this was agreed to, Josiah called me over and made me swear a vow of secrecy with the others.

I did not carry the body. That I was spared. But I helped gather rocks. We filled the trader's pockets with the heaviest of them and lashed more to his feet, then put him in a canoe with Spofford and Big John Biggs. Josiah took Spofford's place in my canoe—I trembled when I saw him come near—and as soon as we'd paddled a quarter mile out, he ordered us to stop. Spofford and Biggs pitched the body over. The moon had risen, and it lit the trader's face as he sank beneath the lake. His cheeks and forehead flashed pale, and then his body turned. The last I saw of him was his hands. Unbound, they floated above his hair, reaching toward me, it seemed, until the darkness finally swallowed them and he was taken by the deep.

We paddled on. I tried to distract my mind from the image of the trader's mute face, from the terrible seeping wound. I could not. As we neared Port Hebron I began to understand the full ramification of what I'd done. Damnation would be upon me. I would be forever locked out of the celestial kingdom. I assumed Josiah had taken Spofford's place in the canoe to tell me just this. But, as if knowing my inner struggle, at that very moment he told me to ease my mind. "You raised your hand to save me," he said as we came past Apostle's Point, "not to take that man's life. He forfeited it. The punishment falls on his soul." He paused, and then he said, "Because of what you've done, I'm raising you to the Order."

I ceased paddling.

"The Order?" I asked. I stared at Josiah's back and waited for him to tell me I had misheard.

"Yes, the Order," he said. "You'll be the first."

I was struck by the pure shock of the honor. The Order! Then, with a jolt, I remembered. My mind thrilled with visions of Dorothea. I saw her, waiting for me in her father's cabin. Bainbridge's thundered words the night of my last visit resounded in my head. I had him. One of the greatest sins, according to *The Book of Truths,* was to break an oath. He couldn't refuse me now.

Once we returned to Port Hebron, the others, tired from the sortie, drifted back to their cabins and cottages with a few mumbled salutations. But I couldn't rest. I rushed across the island to the Bainbridge farm and arrived just as dawn broke. I didn't pause to knock but stepped into the cabin and went straight to Dorothea, who stood at the fire boiling oats. "William!" she said. "You can't be here. My father."

Just then Bainbridge emerged from behind one of the hanging blankets, risen to take his breakfast. "Mr. Ames," he said when he saw me, his voice cold as the gray ice that had covered the island's roads and paths all through winter, so many forgotten months ago.

"Remember your oath, Mr. Bainbridge," I burst out.

He drew his face into a blank of confusion.

"The night you forbade me to court Dorothea, you said you would allow me to propose to her the day I was raised to the Order."

"A figure of conver—"

"You made an oath, Mr. Bainbridge, an oath and a bargain. I have fulfilled my end. This night I was raised to the Order. Now you must let me offer myself to Dorothea."

Dorothea looked to her father. "Is it true?" she asked.

Bainbridge ignored her. Hoping, I imagine, to trap me in a lie, he asked how I'd accomplished such a feat. I told him the version of the story I and the others had sworn to, then added that he could ask Josiah himself if he doubted me. Bainbridge groaned and sat. He put his hand to his forehead and seemed to be deliberating. "Very well," he finally said.

I knelt at Dorothea's feet, and before I could pose the question or even wonder what she might say, she nodded. Her pale cheeks blushed and her dark eyes filled with tears. How strangely the Lord had worked to unite us! Her father stormed out of the cabin, but I was too delighted to pay him any mind. I took hold of Dorothea's hand and kissed it, saying now it was truly mine I would never let it go.

As we crossed the spine of July, high summer reached the island. Side-wheelers began putting in each day, taking on the cordwood we sold them for the run east through the Straits or south to Chicago, and fishing boats arrived in our waters to pack their holds with trout and sturgeon. With the demand on barrels I had few hours free from Pickle's work yard, but those few I spent with Dorothea. Now we were betrothed we were allowed to walk together. Her father absented himself whenever I appeared, and Dorothea and I strolled along the edge of the potato field and sketched our lives, I telling her how someday I would open my violin shop, she telling me how she longed to sail the lakes, to have a boat and explore the wild coasts. In our fantasies we built our house, we named our children, we stood at the rising of the kingdom. Our thoughts were littered with promise. She would close her eyes as we talked and curl her mouth into a grin, resting her cheek on my shoulder. Afterward she would lead me into the wood and let me put my lips to hers, let me touch her cheek and hold her in my arms. My fingertips trembled against her flesh, and I felt again what I had felt the night of my conversion: the island growing within me, the future coming as it should.

Most of my visits passed like this, but on occasion Dorothea would be caught in a dark study. Once I found her sitting in her small flower garden with her arms tight around her skirts, clutching her folded legs to her chest, staring off above the birches. Rather than jump up when she heard me approach, as she usually did, she refused even to turn.

"Dory."

No answer.

I sat beside her, asked about the garden, tried any number of ways to gain her attention until at last she seemed to rise back to herself. She presented me with a smile, and asked if we could go for a walk. Then we strolled and talked as usual, though she ignored my inquiries about the state in which I had found her.

It was after one of these appearances of her shadow—for that is how I called it to myself—that I was asked to Josiah's home. His cottage, the finest on the island, sat apart from town, to the north, and was surrounded by a picket fence and flanked by two six-pounder cannons. Despite being raised to the Order, I'd never been asked to the cottage before, and had spoken to Josiah only a few times since the night of the sortie—mostly in the Temple, where, as the Order's sole member, I performed my one duty, standing guard in a velvet tunic beneath the Arch of the Blood while Josiah prayed.

When I arrived, Josiah's wife, Celia, showed me into his office and brought us glasses of honeyed milk. She was a gray-faced woman five years his senior and rarely left the cottage. It was said, under breath, that the money from her first husband's estate had laid the foundation for our colony. Josiah was at work, writing. Uncertain what to do with myself, I sipped from my glass and looked about the room. Behind Josiah hung a map of the island showing Port Hebron as Zion—the completed Temple, the grid of streets stretching across the island to house the 144,000—and below the map stood shelves of plant specimens, which, I'd heard, Josiah regularly sent to a professor at Union College. The study's window faced onto the harbor, and mounted on its sill was a brass telescope, pointed toward the open lake beyond the bay. The harbor had grown yet busier in the last weeks. Soon, Josiah had told us, the federal gunboat that patrolled the upper lakes was to put in. He was expected to go down and greet her captain.

My eyes had made it as far as a snake coiled in a jar—it sat on the floor, directly beneath the telescope—when the scratching of Josiah's nib stopped and he looked up and said, without preface, "I've learned you are to be married to Dorothea Bainbridge. Is this true?"

I was a trifle surprised, but lost no time in answering. "It is."

"I take an interest in all my charges," he said, "and you especially. I owe you my life."

Josiah drank from his honeyed milk, then proceeded to study me with his gaze. I grew nervous. His eyes pierced mine. The pages of my soul lay open before him. He was testing me somehow, though I wasn't sure why.

When I thought I could stand this gaze no longer, he rose and gave me his holy blessing. "In *The Book of Truths* it is written that a man must not become too attached to the things of this world," he said as he walked me to the door. With that, our meeting was ended, and I left his house as confused over the visit's purpose as when I had entered.

MY NEXT SEVENTH DAY I was assigned to work on the Judge's House, which was being built, as commanded in Josiah's revelation, atop the low slope of Mount Nebo, the island's highest point. The house's plans called for a long five-roomed cottage with a high tower at one end. From the top the Judge, whom Josiah told us to expect daily, would be able to see over the treetops. I enjoyed working on the Judge's House. It was only a mile from the Bainbridge farm, and at the end of the day I would walk there and spend the entire evening with Dorothea.

I was helping a pig farmer named Morris nail planks to the floor of the cottage's porch when Josiah came riding up on his dappled gray. He spoke to our foreman, a man named Pearson, then clicked his tongue and spurred his horse down the southern path, toward New Nazareth. Not long after that we ran out of nails. It was too late in the day to fetch more from Port Hebron, so Pearson gathered us together, gave a prayer of thanksgiving for our labor, and let us go early. The others started their walk back to town, but I set off toward the Bainbridge farm.

I would be an hour early, and I delighted myself with thoughts of Dorothea's surprise. Perhaps I would find her in the garden, weeding away the clover, or in the cabin, tending a stew over the fire. I would sneak behind her, wrap her in my arms, and whisper in her ear.

By the time I reached the Bainbridge farm a fine rain was falling. I paused to pick some dandelions, then took the track through the birch wood and into the potato field. When I came to the clearing, I stopped. Josiah's dapple stood outside the cabin, head down, nibbling at grass. My skin prickled. I thought of Dorothea's shadow and the meeting with Josiah, and a sick chill shuddered through me. I tried to calm myself, to quell the fumbling realization. I recalled Bainbridge's rumored candidacy for eldership, told myself Josiah had come simply to consult with him. But then the cabin door opened, and Josiah walked out. Dorothea stood behind him. Her braids were undone, her dress loose.

My reason gave way like a shattered pane. Josiah and Dorothea hadn't yet seen me, and I made to run to the cabin. Before I could, I was grabbed from behind. It was Bainbridge. He put his hand over my mouth and held me down hidden in the brush while Josiah rode away.

"It was revelation," he whispered into my ear. "It was revelation. I tried to run you off."

As soon as Josiah was gone, Bainbridge let me go. I pushed myself from him, then turned to look at him.

"She's his," Bainbridge said. He shook his head and covered his eyes with his palm. I'd never imagined he could be so abject. "That's why I sent you off. The Lord chose her as one of Josiah's royal concubines, like King David had. He told me we must keep it secret. Then you, with that damned oath. I begged him for a release, to let you marry Dorothea, but he said you can't stop revelation."

I left Bainbridge and went straight to the cabin. Dorothea had gone back inside and I found her at the table. She was staring at the wall, her face drawn into a familiar absence. I called her name, but she didn't turn. Her mother sat beside her, holding her hand and stroking her hair.

I had entered intending to shout, but my heart shivered and the words wouldn't come.

TWO WEEKS LATER the federal gunboat *Superior* was spotted on the horizon. It was now September, a year since my arrival. Summer had begun to ease itself from the lake. Save for one night, I hadn't ventured farther than Pickle's work yard. I had skipped the Sabbath services, had stayed at home on my seventh day. After discovering the truth, I contemplated returning to Baltimore. My father would welcome me back to his shop, and I could take up my old life again. I packed my things into a single bag, counted and recounted the dollars I had left: enough for passage to Detroit. But my rage boiled and wouldn't let me leave. At night, in his corner of the cabin, Pickle mumbled his prayers on my behalf.

Already two ships had put in, the Chicago steamer *Lady of the Lakes* and a fisherman called *Sutton's Fancy*, but the sighting of the *Superior*, with her promise of uniformed sailors, a troop of marines, and a band of fife and drum, caused a stir. Hebronites and passengers from the *Lady of the Lakes*, who'd come ashore while she took on wood for her engines, crowded the docks to watch as the gunboat came past Apostle's Point. I went down to the water, too, but kept back from the others. Stacks of cordwood lined the shore in rows, and from just beyond the end of these I could see the entire breadth of the bay. The sun shone brightly, turning the waves to diamonds, bleaching the sky of its blue. On the docks some of the men held children on their shoulders and waved their hats in salute. Gentile women giggled and pointed at the boat from beneath their parasols. Their pink ribbons and white summer dresses gleamed.

The tableau of cheerfulness was too much. I looked away, and that's when I saw the whiskey traders. Two of them stood among the cordwood stacks. They were got up in broadcloth suits and had trimmed their beards, but I recognized the wildness in them, recognized the slouch that bespoke discomfort with civilized clothes, the brute dullness in their eyes that came from their animal life of sin. Unlike everyone else, they were turned away from the boat and looking toward town, their hands in their pockets.

The one night I had strayed from Pickle's cabin, it had been to go to them. I had taken a canoe and paddled across to the near islands until I saw the glow of one of their camps. They took me captive once they spotted me, held a knife to my throat, pushed me down against the sand. Their eyes glinted in the firelight as they leaned over me. I had not tried to hide, and they asked me what I was playing at. When I told them I had killed their fellow, one of them called for rope. I shouted that I sorrowed for it now. It wasn't a lie, the dead trader's face haunted my dreams. And I said that I regretted having let Josiah live. Curses fell from the hollows of their mouths. Bits of elkhorn hung from the one who brought the rope. They pulled me to the water, made to push me under, but I kept shouting. I told them about the press of the late-summer traffic and the commotion of the federal ship's arrival. There they would have their chance, I said. At that, they released me, and I slipped into Pickle's cabin just before dawn. He stirred when I entered, but didn't wake.

Now I watched the whiskey traders among the cordwood stacks. From Josiah's house one of the six-pounders fired a salute. I turned in time to see him step from his front door. He was to come down to the dock to receive the gunboat's captain in a short ceremony. Following the cannon's salute, the *Superior*'s band struck up a military air. As she came into harbor, the melody carried over the chuffing of her engine and the slap of her side paddle wheel. The men on the pier hurrahed.

The path from Josiah's house to the dock would lead him past me, and he appeared in good spirits as he approached, whistling and nodding, in his freshly brushed coat. A few yards beyond me he would be caught between the whiskey traders and the cordwood. His life would be in their hands. But now, again, it was in mine. I could step forward, could reach out to stop him and save our paradise, broken as it was. Or I could remain still and let it be taken.

A buffet of wind whipped up from the lake. There was a splash, a shout, laughter—someone on the dock had dived into the water.

It was easy. Josiah hadn't yet noticed me. I let him pass, then turned away. I didn't care to watch.

I HEARD THE FIRST SHOT when I was halfway to Pickle's cabin, then three more. By the last the gunboat's band had ceased playing.

A lone scream cut through the stilled crowd, then the air itself seemed to breathe before erupting into a confused, wailing din that spread up from the docks. Someone had lifted Josiah's body and called now for help. Several of my brothers ran past me, on their way to the water. Celia's blanched face emerged from the cottage amid the clamor. I recalled Josiah's telescope and wondered if she had been watching through it.

Pickle came in after dark, hours later. I had last seen him standing on the dock, cheering the *Superior.* Now his boots were caked with mud, his clothes damp with sweat and pricked with burrs. When he saw me in my corner, from which I hadn't shifted since noon, he took a little step back. "I thought you were with the others."

I shook my head.

"We chased those dogs across the island, but they got to their canoe. They're with their fellows. Can't you hear them?"

I'd not noticed the sound before, but now I could make out the whiskey traders' hoots and curses echoing over the water. Pickle sat on his bed, head bowed. Then he convulsed, and I realized he was weeping. I glanced away, at his calendar covered with *x*'s, at my violin hanging in the window, at the lamp glasses black with soot. He had been good to me, and I had cut him from the kingdom.

THE FEDERAL GUNBOAT DEPARTED, the captain having claimed this was none of his affair. The other ships left soon after, and the elders shut themselves in the Temple. Some of the brethren had already abandoned their cabins and made camp on the dock to await the next steamer. By morning the news had reached across the island: God's judgment.

Overnight the sky had turned gray. Thick clouds pressed low against the lake, and cold seeped through the cracks in the cabin's walls. I ignored the breakfast Pickle made, put on my black coat, and walked to the Bainbridge farm, where I found Dorothea's father lifting their trunks onto a borrowed wagon. He saw me, but refused to meet my eye. Dorothea's mother was in the yard, boiling their clothes. She pointed to the clothesline. Dorothea was there, hanging sheets.

I waited for her to turn, but she ignored me. When the last sheet was hung she began adjusting the first, careful not to come near where I stood. Her manner made me anxious, but at the same time I became angry. Something promised me was being withheld.

"You're free," I said. "We can marry."

"After what you saw? After everything?" she said. She showed me her face and it was twisted in anguish. "It's too late."

"It's not," I said. "I promise, I'll forget everything." I took her, held her in my arms. "Meet me tonight at the Judge's House," I said. "Will you?" Only when she nodded did I let her go.

All through the first hours of night I paced the timber skeleton of the Judge's House. I imagined Dorothea waiting for her father to fall asleep, or writing a long letter to her mother. But as the night grew longer, I began to fear the worst. Finally I went back to the farm. It was empty, and at the sight a dizziness rippled up from my feet. I raced to Port Hebron and arrived an hour after dawn, in time to see a steamer leaving the bay. I searched among the dock camp that now spread along the shore, but Dorothea wasn't there. After questioning a few acquaintances, I ran into Spofford, who told me he'd seen the Bainbridges board the boat. I looked out over the water and felt the bruises of my heart turn black.

I returned to Pickle's cabin. When Pickle came in he told me that two of the elders had fled the island, taking the sacred books and the treasury with them, and that Celia had shut herself in the cottage; Josiah's body lay spread on the dining table, and she refused to let him be buried. I stayed at the window. At night the whiskey traders returned to the bay in their canoes. Their shouting stirred me like a summons.

A day later another steamer put in. Pickle gathered his belongings into two carpetbags. He offered to pay my passage, but I told him I wasn't leaving.

He stood in the doorway. "It's all gone," he said.

I told him my decision had been made, and when he asked what I meant, I got up, took my violin from the window, offered it to him, and bid him go.

FOR A WEEK LONGER, as the island cleared, I stayed in the cabin. I did not shave, nor did I visit the bathhouse, which was shut up now, anyway. I ate our last stores of food—hungrily, greedily, as if both nursing the wound within and feeding the fever that spread through my veins. At the end of the week I opened the door and stepped outside. By now the streets were empty. The whiskey traders had remained in their camps, and silence had descended, encasing every building in Port Hebron in a thin glass shell. The few noises were the sharper for it: a rodent scurrying from the sight of me, the crackle of a fire burning unchecked. Even the scent of the air was changed, carrying nothing but a tinge of smoke. In this strange, vacant quiet I felt my new beard. I searched abandoned cabins and wrapped myself in the furs and hides left behind. I bent to the ground and darkened my cheeks with mud. Then, at last, I went down to the water and yelled for my new brothers to come.

ERASER

Two Deadly Fish

I lift up the lid of the livewell and look inside. A couple fish—bass, largemouth—sit in place, not really swimming.

"What's up, fish?" I say.

The fish open their mouths and close them, which is about all they do. You can't tell by looking at them, but they're poisoned. Like, if you eat too many, you go blind, or crazy, or you become sterile or some shit. They've got signs at the pier and boat ramp, no more than two fish a week. It's the fishes' revenge, I guess, even though it's really the big power plant that sits on the side of the lake that does it.

"Fish don't need hassling," my stepfather says to no one, meaning me.

I close the lid.

Usually, whenever my stepfather wants to tell me something, he'll make some general comment or filter what he's got to say through my mom instead of just talk to me. Not that I'm complaining.

I go sit behind the steering wheel and look at the screen mounted there. It shows how deep the lake is below the boat, and the size of any fish passing below. I wonder if it would show a dead body, if there's a picture programmed in it for that. See, son, a dad'll say, tapping on the screen, that's a child. We only need the small net.

"Monster off the port bow!" I shout when a large fish swims on-screen, to be helpful.

My stepfather ignores me.

My mom reads her book.

The fish swims away.

A Choice of Ends

I don't like to fish. I just don't. Maybe it's genetic. My dad never fished, and we were never big on any of the typical father-son stuff. Like the one time I dragged him outside to play catch, the ball missed my glove on the first throw and bounced off my skull and over the fence.

Instead, my dad used to take me to Civil War battlefields, re-enactments, history talks where Minié balls and pottery shards were passed around the audience of old people and us. He left three years ago, when I was nine. He got a new job in Shreveport and told my mom he needed to start over in the city. Which is pretty funny. I mean, have you been to Shreveport?

Once, before I discovered I don't like to fish, I was baiting my hook with a cricket. A live cricket. I, who was never one of those boys that likes torturing insects or cats or anything, could not get around the central fact of this action: the sticking of the hook through the cricket's (live!) abdomen. The cricket jumped in my fingers, twitching its legs. I brought the hook to its side, pushed a little, then my fingers loosened and the cricket got away. Chasing it, I knocked over the carton of crickets, a dozen more got out, and the one I was chasing jumped into the lake. So there you go. Drowning versus impaling.

If given the choice, I think I'd do the same.

Exhibit A

A while back my stepfather was cooking dinner when he told me to drop a piece of chicken into the Fry Daddy.

"Gotta learn how to cook," he said, and so like an idiot I went over and took a drumstick and dropped it in. When the oil popped I jerked my hand back and he said, "Scared?"

Right then I knew I'd screwed up, that I should have just kept walking out of the kitchen. He hummed something menacing—a hash-up of *Jaws*—and grabbed my wrist, forcing my hand to the hot oil until it was just an inch from the fizzing surface. When I finally pulled my hand loose, he said, "Lighten up."

I didn't say anything, just laughed like I'd been in on the joke from the beginning.

There's still a round brown scar on the back of my hand from where the oil spattered.

The Water's Return

My stepfather moves the boat over to the bridge to fish for perch. From here you can see the dam. Little orange buoys mark where you're not supposed to cross. I imagine a boat accidentally drifting in there, its outboard burning against the strain, a whole family with their rods and lunch-meat sandwiches being pulled in, under and through the turbines.

"Kids, I'm so, so sorry," the father says, on his knees.

"I'm sorry, too," the mother says.

"We are full of regret," they both say as they weep.

My mom says, "Why don't you fish a little?" She puts down her book and picks up her rod.

I tell her there's no way I'm putting another cricket on a hook.

My stepfather casts his line out. He and my mom married two years ago. When he came into the family, it's like he saw us as a bunch of softies he needed to toughen up. "Y'all need to get outside more," he'd say. "See the sun." But where he tanned, we burned, and even though he took us camping and fishing and paid for us to go on horse rides, none of it stuck. My stepfather must have been surprised when he got me. All along he must have wanted a son to teach all this crap to, and there I was—a chubby kid who'd rather watch *The Price Is Right* while downing a bag of Cheetos than gut an animal. I can't say I blame him for being disappointed.

"Put a worm on it then," my mom says.

I say okay and get one of the rubber worms from the tackle box. I pick a green one with sparkles. Then I cast and the line actually goes out a respectable distance. I take my time reeling it in, stopping and starting the line in erratic jiggles to make my worm more lifelike. It probably makes my worm look like it's got epilepsy. All part of the plan, I say half aloud. What fish could resist the easy prey of an epileptic worm?

While I'm reeling in, I watch the lake. It's pretty new, only about ten or fifteen years old. There aren't any real lakes in Texas—they're all built with dams. People used to live on the bottom when the lakes were still farms and ranches. It must be awkward for their ghosts, I think. To find fish swimming in and out of where they used to sleep.

My science teacher, Mr. Homeniuk, says Texas was covered by a sea in prehistoric times. So maybe all these new lakes do belong here. Maybe we're the ones in the wrong place.

A Bad Habit

At school, I get good grades. Like, really good grades. I mean, I've still got five years to screw up, but my grades are good enough that some of my teachers are already talking college.

In math class I don't have to listen too much because the work comes easy. One day I was bored and playing around with my textbook and accidentally marked one of the pages with my pen. So I took my pencil and—careful, hiding what I was doing from Mrs. Pickett so I wouldn't get into any trouble—erased the pen mark. It came off, but so did the lower half of a fraction. Where the ink and denominator had been, there was just blank page. I erased the other numbers. They disappeared. Without a trace.

At first I was scared. This was *tampering with school property*, the thing our principals are always getting angry about. But then it was like, hey, they'll never catch me. They still don't know who set the practice field on fire.

During class I erase more numbers. Not too many—not enough to tip off the next poor kid who gets the book, whose little world won't add up. And you have to do it right. Like if the number's 14, you don't erase the 4. That's just stupid. You erase the 1. Sometimes I turn to the answers and erase a couple numbers there, too.

Exhibit B

A month ago we were at a barbecue at one of my stepfather's friends' houses. These people bred Rottweilers in their backyard, and while we were there the barking never stopped. "You get used to it," my stepfather's friend said. He was a short man without a neck, like a movie gangster, and he called all of the dogs Beauty. He was showing them off when one of the dogs, Beauty number 4, bit at me through the cage, her teeth snagging my shirt.

I could already hear my stepfather's comment. "Guess she likes fat." So I acted like I didn't even notice and picked up a stick and poked at the dog through the cage's wires, just to mess with it, to show I knew which side of the cage I was on. It was the kind of thing my stepfather would do, I thought, but before I could even touch Beauty's side he came and grabbed the stick out of my hand and asked what the hell I was thinking. Then he shook his head like I was stupid and walked away.

Later, when no one was looking, I grabbed a hotdog and set it outside the cage where Beauty couldn't reach it. I watched as she pressed her nose against the wires and whined, like that would make the hotdog roll closer. She strained and strained, and I didn't do anything to help her.

The Train to Nowhere

My line catches and for half a second I think I've got a fish. But then there's no pull and I reel the line in, dragging up a beard of hydrilla. I tug it off the hook and throw it back into the lake. Hydrilla's like seaweed, except it grows in the lake. So lakeweed, I guess. It's not supposed to be here. It accidentally came in on someone's boat, or someone brought it here to kill off something else, and now it fills the lake, wrapping itself around outboards, fishing lures, your legs and arms if you actually go for a swim in this toxic dump.

"Okay. I fished," I say.

"You see that," my stepfather says to my mom. And through her to me, of course. At first I think he's talking about my defeatism, as he calls it, and going to say something about how kids today (meaning me) need more discipline, but then I see he's pointing at the shore. He does this a lot, wherever we go. Spots wildlife like he's our hunting guide. Part of that whole toughening-us-up scheme, I guess. So if me and my mom ever have to survive on our own in the woods or something, we can spot animals. Which will comfort us, I suppose, as we die of starvation.

"I don't see it. What?" my mom says. She's got this stupid pink hat on—like a baseball cap but with an oversized bill—that ties in the back with a bow, and the bow jiggles as she jerks her head looking up and down the shore.

"A nutria," my stepfather says. "By that log. Now it's gone into the water."

I don't even know what a nutria is.

"Oh, shoot," my mom says. She's always disappointed when she doesn't see something my stepfather points out, like it's this big deal. And for half a second I think, hey, maybe she's right. Maybe I'm the idiot for not paying attention. Maybe I should be staring at nutrias after all.

Not long after my dad moved to Shreveport, he quit his job and started selling belt buckles and canteens at reenactments. He said it was his dream. He grew a beard, started dressing up like he was in a tintype and working on a book about some guy named Corporal Edwards who fought in the Civil War. He told me all this in a letter, said he was going to Xerox the book himself and sell it for five dollars. But I haven't seen it yet.

Behind me I hear a whistle and I turn to look at the power plant. A little train runs from the plant to somewhere else—I don't know where—and brings back coal. Maybe there's a coal mine nearby, though in school when they gave us maps with little pictures showing Texas's natural resources, I didn't see a coal nugget. An oil derrick, yes. A cow, yes. A cotton boll, yes. But no coal nugget. So maybe it's just a stockpile of coal this train goes to. Anyway, the train only runs back and forth from the plant to wherever the coal comes from. It does this all day and all night too, I guess. Right now it's headed to the power plant, its cars filled to the top with coal.

I point to the train. "You see that?"

No one looks.

The Wind in My Hair

My favorite part of a fishing trip—yes, I do have a favorite part—is when we speed across the lake to find a spot to fish or speed back to the boat ramp. I sit up front and let the wind hit me. I like going places fast, even if it's not really anyplace I want to go. Sometimes I imagine rolling off the boat when we're speeding across the lake. Balling up my legs and wrapping my arms around them, then tumbling off. It would hurt, I know. I've gone tubing before, and every time I fell off the tube it was like someone slapping me in the gut, hard, before I sank into the water.

But my fear isn't how it'll hurt when I land on the water. It's the propeller. What if I somehow roll the wrong way, get sucked under the boat and shredded by the propeller? It's a small propeller, sure, but it scares me enough.

Still, it would be nice to hear my mom scream in worry. It would be nice for my stepfather to stop the boat to save me.

Exhibit C

Just last week we were at a different lake, camping, when my stepfather said, "Heads up!" and pushed me underwater. I flailed, the dirty water flooding my nostrils and my mouth as I tried to scream.

"Don't be such a pantywaist," he said when he let me up. "I was just horsing around."

I told him I wasn't scared, that he was too quick, I didn't have enough time. Which was a big lie, of course. I went after him to grab him, to pull him under. This was a rare sight: me trying. But he just looked at me and said it was too late. And it's like I finally knew. Of course I could never win. So I said I didn't give a shit. His back was turned, and I muttered it, but I meant it. I swam some more, my feet catching at tree roots, and didn't give a shit.

A Narrow Escape

In math class, I was erasing more numbers when Mrs. Pickett called my name. I'd been taking too many chances. Like, I'd erase a whole problem, which is just stupid because it shows my hand. I mean, when you look from problem eight to problem ten and see this huge blank space in between, it doesn't take a genius to figure out something's off.

I started to sweat. Mrs. Pickett was looking at me, and the class was quiet.

"Could you come up to the board and help Jason with this problem?"

Oh. That's all. "Sure," I said.

At the board, Jason breathed in my ear and whispered "pussy-licker" at me while I finished his problem.

I whispered, "You wish," and only when I sat down did I realize the perfect comeback. You fucking bet I am. I said it now under my breath—"You fucking bet I am"—and Jenna Blalock, who's already thirteen, flirts with everyone, and has the third-biggest tits in our grade, turned around, her eyes wide in mock horror.

Later, during lunch, I thought of what I'd say if Mrs. Pickett ever did catch me. It's perfect. It's in every after-school special and probably every teacher's student psychology handbook. "What is this?" she'll say, pointing to some empty spaces. "That," I'll say, "is a cry for help."

Back to Port

I've got a sunburn now, so there's that. My stepfather puts another fish in the livewell, ripping the hook out of its jaw like it's nothing, and then decides it's time to go home. My mom's been ready for a few minutes. I've been ready for hours.

I help prepare the boat, though no one asks me, taking down the raised fishing seats so they screw in level with the deck. Then I sit in the one up front.

My stepfather heads us back toward the boat ramp, opening up the motor when we get to the part of the lake where the hydrilla isn't so bad. The boat bounces a couple times when we cross some-one else's wake, and then we round a bend and come in sight of the beach, where the Army Corps of Engineers trucked in sand so people can swim and play in a lake that poisons fish.

"You're going to help me clean these bass," he shouts up to me, and all of a sudden I'm sick of it, I'm so sick of it. He knows I hate cleaning fish: the dead scales sticking to my fingers, the fish blood on my hands. And of course my mom's just sitting there, saying nothing.

Once, when I wrote to my dad and told him how crappy things were and begged him to let me stay with him, he wrote back that life is about adjustment. I couldn't tell if he was talking about me or himself. He went on about Corporal Edwards, saying how when he returned home from the war, he found raccoons nesting in his cabin, his wife run off to New Orleans. Sure, being adjusted is easy if you're dead, I thought, and in some book.

The shore's rushing toward us, and I'm about to mouth off when it comes to me, the daydream from my other fishing trips. Me tumbling over the side, my mom and my stepfather seeing it all and springing into action to save me. I picture how they'll worry, the quick sad flash in their faces. And then it's like, why not? I mean, what if this is the thing, the one thing that'll make everything else okay? And then it's like I can't not do it. I look around. The lake's clear. I think about it, and then I stop thinking about it. I ball my legs and grip my knees, and I go.

Halfway over, I hear my mom shriek. I'm in the air, and my stepfather's killed the engine. For a split second it's like it's all falling into place. They're watching, I know they're watching, and I want to keep this moment forever, the quiet, the smell of the lake below me, the wind whipping my hair, everything belonging, me belonging, just like I wanted.

Then I glance back, and it's lost. They haven't seen me at all. That pink hat has flown off my mom's head—that's why my stepfather stopped the boat—and they're looking the other way, watching as the hat floats on a breeze. And it's like, really? Really? I take a breath, but before I can shout to them, the lake reaches up to slap me and pull me in, and I'm gone.

AT BOQUILLAS

THEY WERE HIKING DOWN THE HILL when they first heard the singing—a distant, lone man's voice that seemed to echo off the river, or maybe off the canyon walls that rose at the trail's end. Shelly said she thought the singing might be a radio, and Josh, her husband, said he wasn't sure.

The hike was short, just over a half mile from the parking lot to the opening of Boquillas Canyon, where you were supposed to stop and watch the Rio Grande pouring between the sheer cliffs. The singing continued as they descended to the river's edge, where the reeds kept them from seeing anything but the trail itself and the sky above. *Cuando,* the voice said, pleading.

"Probably one of those guys in the shelter," Josh said. At the top of the hill, they had looked across the river and seen a small shelter made of sticks with four Mexican men squatting beneath it. Shelly had felt a pang of guilt while studying them—for being invasive, for being the privileged white woman peering into someone else's hardscrabble life—but she couldn't help looking. Mexico itself didn't so much fascinate her as did the simple notion of a wholly foreign place just across the river.

"They were just sitting," she said now, of the men in the shelter. They hiked on. The trail bent and rose. Ahead of them the reeds and brush cleared, and in the trail's path lay a row of painted walking sticks and colored crystals on a blanket. In front of the blanket sat a milk jug weighted with change and bills. Shelly guessed now the job of the men in the hut—to run across and snatch the goods and the day's takings if the border patrol came over the hill. On the far side of the river a little metal boat was tied up. She discovered, too, the source of the singing.

Near the boat a man stood on the sandy bank, serenading them. He looked about fifty, wore jeans and a green shirt, and had binoculars at his eyes, alternately watching them and then turning to watch the hill, to see if anyone else was coming over. Beside the jug was a plain rock, painted with the words: *The Mexican Singing Victor. Your Donations Help Buy Supplies for the School Childrens.*

Shelly stopped and took a dollar from her pocket and put it in the jug. *"Gracias,"* the Mexican Singing Victor called across the river. It was only about thirty feet wide, and shallow. Shelly waved her hand and then looked up toward the rising canyon walls.

"Why'd you do that?" Josh said with a slight scowl.

"Why not?"

"There's border agents in the parking lot," he said. "The signs said not to give those guys money."

"Please," Shelly said, coming up to him and then passing by. Josh didn't say anything, just stood behind, giving her room. Shelly had learned over the years how Josh hated public fights, even though it was usually he who started them. She didn't mind the Singing Victor seeing them. But Josh wouldn't speak, and later, she knew, if he returned to the fight in the safe confines of their car or their tent, he would say that he'd felt the man's eyes pressing into him. When she turned around, Josh was walking with his hands in his pockets, affecting calm, and Victor was watching the hill. He'd stopped singing now that he had his dollar.

THEY HAD SPENT THE WEEK IN FAR WEST TEXAS, the Trans-Pecos, hiking the Guadalupes and then driving down to Big Bend. This was their fifth year of marriage, and the trip was to mark their return to normalcy—they'd just taken twelve weeks of counseling after Shelly had caught Josh with his chubby, moonfaced student teacher, Karleen. Shelly had come to the school to bring him dinner, a surprise, and found the two clutching each other in Josh's classroom. They parted, and the girl seemed about to speak, or to cry, but at Shelly's stare she ran out of the room, bumping into a desk and toppling a box of pencils. How stupid she looked, Shelly thought, that stupid girl. It was the only thing she let herself think. Already the year had been hard—Shelly had lost her teaching job because of the school district's funding cuts.

"Three months," Josh said before she asked. He'd sat in one of the student desks and put his face in his hands. "God, I'm sorry."

"Shit," Shelly said in disbelief, the hurt still welling up as she sat at another desk. "I mean, shit."

"We stayed late putting up posters," Josh said. He stared at his desktop. A student, Shelly saw, had carved *cock* into the desk and colored the gouges with blue pen. "And it just happened, and then kept happening."

"Just happened?" Shelley yelled. "I'm supposed to believe that? One minute you're tacking a poster to the wall, and the next you've got your dick inside her?"

The smell of fried catfish and hush puppies rose from the food containers in the plastic bag. "I'll do whatever you want," Josh said.

Shelly wasn't sure what to say. The anger made it hard to think. It was something hot pressing against her neck and her temples, like when her mother used to grab her. "Do you still love me?"

Josh looked up at her quickly. "Of course," he said. "Yes."

And so they had gone to marriage counseling. The counselor had told Josh to move out of the house, that Shelly could only let him back in when she trusted him. And Josh had to keep his cell phone with him, turned on at all times so Shelly could call him whenever she wanted, to see what he was doing. Josh also had to give Shelly a full daily schedule.

"I feel like a science project," Josh had said, trying for a laugh.

"You broke our trust," Shelly said, her voice sharp. "This is serious. You broke it, and now you have to earn it back."

After two months, Shelly felt he had, and asked him to move back in. By the end of the counseling, they seemed well on the path together—that's how Shelly thought of their marriage now, following that last session, as a path going up a hill, behind which the sun was rising.

LOOKING AT THE RIVER, Shelly pictured a dotted line running down its middle.

"It's weird," she said, "that that's another country over there, only a few feet away, that we can see it, can walk to it—"

"But we can't," Josh said. "That's just it." He looked over to the canyon, up the hill behind them. "I bet there's a border agent up there somewhere, talking with the ones in the lot. You go over that river, you can't cross back, not unless you go a hundred miles either way to a border crossing."

She didn't mean she wanted to go over; she was just talking. "I'm only saying it's stupid. It's just right there." She looked at the brown river. It wasn't deep—a few feet at most. "It's nothing. I could run there and back in two seconds."

Across the river the reeds were green, like the ones on their side, and a burro was nosing behind a tall bush, which seemed too clichéd to be true, the burro, but there it was. The four men were still under their stick shelter, and Victor was still watching the hill for the next tourists.

"I'm just saying it's dumb, is all."

Josh ignored her, and they walked the last few yards toward the canyon without speaking. The trail ended where a giant mound of sand spilled from the canyon's wall. Past this the river bank turned in, closed against the cliffs, and you couldn't go any farther. They stood there, at the bank, peering at the canyon rising above them in a tight V of red and tan stone. Beneath the usual rote fascination, Shelly felt a sudden prickle of sadness. Someday she and everything around her would lie pressed under another layer of rock, that's what the canyon said to her.

Shelly looked again at Josh. "Come on, let's do it," she said, taking Josh's hand. "Just run there and back. No one's here except Singing Victor and his cronies." She nodded toward the shelter.

"Why?" Josh said, pulling his hand free. "What does that prove?"

"Nothing. Just how stupid everything is, I guess."

"I don't want to end up in Mexican prison."

"God, don't be this way. Come on. We just go there and back, together."

"But those guys," Josh said, looking at the shelter. "I bet they're waiting for that. They'll kidnap us or rob us or something."

"No they won't," Shelly said. "That's stupid. Please, it'll be like our renewal."

"Renewal," Josh said.

She took his hand and tried to pull him with her, but he slipped out of her grasp, and she was off, dashing across the river, the water splashing up to her knees, and then she was on the other side. She turned and looked back at Josh, standing there, mopey, and then she looked at the canyon wall, then over at the green river reeds the trail had cut through. It was strange, now, looking at her own country across the way. She looked at Victor, who was looking at her, then turned back to face Josh. Her legs were damp. The wind coming from the canyon made them feel cool. Nothing had happened. Maybe people did this every day.

"Come on!" she shouted over the river's muddy purling, but Josh just stood there.

SHELLY'S FATHER, a preacher, had given up the ministry some years back. He worked at a kiosk in a Dallas mall hustling cell phones, and lived in an upstairs apartment off the freeway. Shelly's mother had left five years before, settling in Phoenix with a chiropractor and calling Shelly every few months or so to make sure she was still alive—that's what she actually said, laughing her new dry desert laugh. Their marriage had always been one of silence, kept in place for the benefit of the small congregation of Highpoint Baptist, which occupied a metal-sided building between a bank branch and a gas station. Shelly feared that her parents' marriage, which had crumbled so soon after her wedding, would somehow corrupt her own, and that first year she had wept often into Josh's lap, hugging him tight and saying, "Don't leave me, I'll never leave you, please don't leave me." She was so scared then that someday he would, or she would. It seemed to be the natural order of things.

But Josh, Shelly soon saw, never worried, even with her holding close to him and crying in his lap. He was so caught up with the idea of himself, he seemed unable even to consider the fact that any distance could grow between them, no matter how much he pushed and pushed. True, he could be sweet and loving, but once, when she told him about how she wanted a big yard where she'd grow vegetables and raise chickens, he laughed and said, "You have such small dreams." She felt the hurt for months. Still, she thought, maybe he was right. Lately he'd been spending his spare time in the bedroom they'd made into his study, determined to find the investment that would make them rich. He had a stack of prospectuses from Brazilian and Philippine companies, the cheap ink on their onionskin pages staining his fingers.

A couple nights before they left for West Texas, Josh cornered Shelly in the apartment's kitchen and heatedly related his new plan: they would cash out her retirement fund (it was just sitting there now she'd been laid off, he said) and put it in a Philippine mining company he'd found. She knew nothing would come of it. Before his investing phase, he'd taken art classes at night and ended up with two drawings in a show at the community center in Grapevine. For a month after the show he'd talked of moving to the Virgin Islands, where he'd paint while she taught, and then the art phase had fizzled. But what struck her as she stood in the kitchen, cradling a mug of coffee while he gesticulated, was that his plans never allowed much room for her beyond ponying up money or holding the day job. She'd never realized that before— and she wasn't asking for much, after all, only a yard and chickens. It was then, leaning against the refrigerator as she sipped her coffee, pretending to listen as Josh talked about manganese, that she first imagined life on her own, held that possibility against the vision of the path with the sun behind it. The path seemed less inviting now.

Standing in the kitchen, Josh had been looking at her, waiting for an answer to a question she hadn't heard. She put away her meandering thoughts and asked him to repeat what he'd said. Because this too she'd learned from her parents' marriage: that you can make a mistake and not know it for years and years. And even more terrifying, never learn what the mistake was, just feel its misery coming down on you for the remainder of your life. Sometimes her father claimed that marrying her mother was the mistake, other times it was letting her go. Mostly they didn't discuss it.

SHELLY WALKED OVER TO THE BURRO. The animal was nosing at the roots of a small tree, pulling up bits of grass. When she got close, it huffed and trotted away a few feet. Victor and the other men weren't paying attention to her now—Victor was watching the trail with his binoculars.

"Come back!" Josh shouted over the river. He was flapping his hand, motioning for her to cross. At first she thought he was only embarrassed, but now she saw he was scared. *"Please."*

Then Victor started singing again. More people were coming down the trail. Fine, she thought, and crashed through the water once more, the river silky and cool, the current pushing her a little as she crossed to her husband's side. It was as simple as she'd said.

No one had leapt out at her, no sharpshooter hidden in the canyon face had fired. Josh hugged her, more tightly than usual, but her clasp was weaker, and she pulled away first.

"What's the big deal?" she said. Victor was still singing, and, over Josh's shoulder, she could see the passel of tourists coming down the hill, a fat man in a floppy hat at their head.

AFTER THE HIKE they drove over to the camp store, where Josh waited while Shelly took a pay-shower. The water was good and hot, and when she finished she dried herself with one of the towels they'd brought. She dressed and then went outside and sat under the metal awning, her hair still wet. She thought about the big lawn, the chickens running underfoot as she went to her tomato plants, basket in hand. Last week a friend from college had told her about an opening at her school in Waxahachie.

The day was in its full heat, but the shade made it pleasant, and every few seconds a breeze rose, coming across the parking lot and empty campsites. No one camped near the river. Everyone, like them, was up in the Chisos Basin, with the red mountains rising around them, where it was cooler. Josh sat next to her. Together they watched a roadrunner trot across the asphalt, then a rabbit came out from some brush and gnawed on a dandelion.

Later, at the campsite, Josh cooked a can of Dinty Moore over the propane stove. When the stew was warm, he poured it into their plastic bowls, passing one to Shelly. She took her spoon, lifted a chunk of meat to her lips, cooled it with her breath, then ate.

"I'm leaving when we get back," she said after she swallowed.

"What?" Josh said. They had neighbors—a couple with a back-packing tent on one side, three middle-aged men in a camper on the other—and she could tell what Josh was thinking. His face was darkening. *Not here,* he wanted to say. *Not now.* He wanted her to grin and say it was a joke. But she said nothing and finished the Dinty Moore. He would carry his stunned, sick heart through the next hours in silence, she knew, and then, once they were alone again, in their tent, and the night was finally quiet, their loud, beer-drinking neighbors safely retreated to their RV, he would try to wake her, whisper her back, believing it that simple, and she'd keep her eyes shut and pretend to be asleep.

TAYOPA

MOTA STUDIED THE MAP as the viceroy's plump, pink finger traced the line of peaks into the far reaches of the northwestern frontier.

"Here," the viceroy said, stopping his finger in a wide stretch of empty parchment. "This is where he says it is."

The viceroy was sitting in his sedan chair, held above the greenest lawn in all of New Spain by a pair of smooth-skinned guinea bucks. Women in meringue-pale dresses strolled past, followed by dandies with needle-thin swords at their waists. Parrots and quetzals squawked in brass cages hung among the trees, stretched their feathers against the wire bars.

"And you believe him, Excellency?" Mota asked.

"He gave me proof," the viceroy said. "Listen. Ninety pesos to the quintal, sixty thousand marks of silver a year. The mine is too rich to ignore." He leaned farther out, causing the front bearer's knees to buckle, and tapped Mota on the chest. "I want you to claim it."

MOTA HAD BEEN AN INSPECTOR OF MINES for the Royal Audiencia for ten years. It was not the career he had intended for himself. At Salamanca his sole friend, the third son of the Duke of Córdoba, had fed him stories of the New World: ribbons of ore, impatient creole virgins, the moon hanging low above a hacienda. So he had come, securing a minor post copying letters in the Audiencia and envisioning a future that already seemed set. He would become rich without thinking and live out his days growing fat in a creole palace, tickling his mistress each night while his wife whelped a child a year. Debarking at Veracruz, he had bribed the customs men and the men from the Holy Office—whose long fingers spidered every passenger's books—so that he might hurry toward this new life in the city of Mexico.

He'd started off well. Within six months he'd made a good match, María Isabel, the seventeen-year-old daughter of a wine merchant. He'd seen her at a ball, standing behind a knot of protective old women, and her dark eyes, her willowy figure, her quiet manner had seemed to hold the secret to his happiness. He wrote letters and had them spirited to her room, spent nights hunched beneath her window. One evening a servant bumped into him in the street and pressed a handkerchief in his hand. It was María Isabel's, and it contained a note in which she confessed that his constant, sorrowful figure had unlatched her soul.

More letters were exchanged. Mota saw María Isabel at other balls, trailed her during her afternoon walks. He pleaded with her father, and after a month of pressing his case he secured the man's approval. Then, a week before they were to marry, Mota bribed the cook to sicken María Isabel's duenna, so that he might climb through his waiting love's window and claim her virginity. He and María Isabel lay together in her great bed with its silk-trimmed sheets until the hour before dawn, giggling as they listened to old Rosita curse and retch. A day later, though, María Isabel broke into sweats, and by the morning set for their wedding she was wrapped in lace and laid in her grave. The surgeon said the disease had risen from the lake in a fume, but Mota blamed himself. He was twenty-two. Locked in his tiny, rented room for five days, he wept until he felt his heart turn brittle. Then he went to the president of the Audiencia and begged for a job that would send him from the city, and the president gave him a mine to audit at Cuencamé.

THE VICEROY HAD TOLD MOTA he would find his guide waiting at the *pulquería* Hijas de Hernández, and it was there Mota went after he left the Alameda. The *pulquería* stood alongside a canal in the southeastern quarter of the city, behind the Convent of La Merced. Indian bargemen and idle creoles sat in its court, shaded by lemon trees as they watched leaves float toward the weir. Their watching was intense, punctuated by shouts—wagers had been placed on each leaf's progress.

Inside the *pulquería,* most of the tables were empty, and those that weren't were occupied by slouched loners or whisperers craned over their drinks. One of Hernández's gawky daughters leaned against the bar, her face lit by a feeble shaft of sun. Alongside the far wall sat a man with the distinct look of a freshly bathed vagrant, his clothes new, his hair washed and combed, yet a nimbus of filth staining his person. His hand rested on a half-empty carafe.

Mota crossed the room toward him. "You are Father Pascual?" he asked. The previous morning, so Mota had learned, a man in tattered black robes calling himself by this name had taken the viceroy's arm as he was leaving the cathedral. He had claimed to be a fugitive from Tayopa, said he had lived in hiding for two years, and offered, for a sizable sum, to guide a party back through the wilderness.

"I am," the vagrant said, and gestured to the table's empty chair. The man looked no older than Mota, but he was balding, his skin calloused and burnt, and he had mummied, claw-like hands. Mota sat and, keeping his voice low, said, "I will get straight to it. You say you come from Tayopa."

Father Pascual bowed in acknowledgment.

"Do you have a map?"

"Here," Father Pascual said as he tapped the left side of his forehead.

"Tell me, then, are the stories true? You Jesuits, your Yaqui slaves, bells struck in silver and gold?"

"Much of it is true," Father Pascual said.

Mota took the carafe of pulque, tipped some into one of the spare glasses sitting on the table, and sipped. His throat burned.

"Why did you leave?"

"I had my reasons."

"All right, so tell me how."

"By night, by accident, and by terror."

Worry swelled like a cloud beneath Mota's stomach. The man shifted, turned, refused him even the slightest hint of solid truth. "You must give me a reason to trust you," Mota said.

Father Pascual looked at him for a moment, then took a silk bundle from his pocket, laid it on the table, and unwrapped a dull, dung-colored rock streaked with the purest vein of silver Mota had ever seen.

"You could have gotten that from anywhere," Mota said.

"Please. You know there's no silver like this left in the New World. Except, of course, where I took it from."

Mota felt his mouth turn dry. "Dawn," he said as Father Pascual put away the rock. "The western causeway. I'll have a mule ready for you."

Mota had arrived at Cuencamé just four weeks after María Isabel's death, still steeped in his sorrow, the memories of María Isabel continuing each day to leach into his blood. A branch of the mine had collapsed, and the low, steady toll of the church's bell summoned coffin sellers to the mine's iron gate, where already a horde of desperate men clamored for the dead men's places. They shoved against widows, and two of the strivers toppled an unclaimed corpse. Mota watched with a mixture of fascination and disgust. Here beat the true pulse of the New World. Here its promises of happiness were given the lie, here the earth opened, loosing the upper chambers of Hell, and stripped men of all falsity.

When, a month later, Mota returned from Cuencamé with his audits, he asked the president of the Audiencia for another mine.

After his meeting with Father Pascual, Mota spent the evening rousing men for the expedition. Among the few in the city he trusted, he found three willing to go. The first was Baltazar, a half-Chichimec with a bull neck who'd once guided *conductas* through the Yucatán and had a skillful way with mules and the various necessities of camp life. The second was El Sepo, a hulking, muscled mulatto who wore gold rings etched with skulls on his fingers, wrote poetry in a little pigskin book, and was an expert tracker and fighter. The last was Fernando, a young, bespectacled creole scholar who always brought with him a satchel of brass instruments fashioned in Leyden and a large sketchbook complete with inks and watercolors for the making of maps and prospects. Mota hadn't seen any of the three for months, and when he told them where they were going each one laughed and shook his head until Mota showed him the viceroy's order with its promise of pay. Now all three waited with him at the end of the western causeway. Baltazar fiddled with the packs and hummed a tune from the city's most recent *mascarada,* Fernando tested one of his Dutch glasses, and El Sepo frowned and crossed out lines in his pigskin book. Already the sun had risen an inch over the low eastern mountains, and Father Pascual was nowhere to be seen. Mota sat on his horse, attempted to stifle his nerves as he watched the city. Mexico seemed a storyteller's vision floating in the middle of its lake, lashed to the land by narrow bridges and causeways, its bell towers and palms and poplars caught in the blue smoke of morning. But then Mota caught sight of a street cleaner pulling his cart of furred corpses; he turned away, remembering the feel of María Isabel's cold, dead hand.

When Father Pascual at last arrived, jogging across the causeway, he shouted his apologies. The man was wearing the same clothes as the day before and carried nothing but a sackcloth bag, stained and worn to a shine at its folds. At Mota's command Baltazar gave the ex-Jesuit a mule and the party set out.

THE FIRST STAGE OF THEIR JOURNEY, from Mexico to Zacatecas, was the easiest. The road was a smooth, tended highway that ran northwest through long-settled country, passing tidy villages, each with its bell tower and public garden, and taverns with bright wooden signs. Farmers in carts trundled by, forced aside at times by guard wagons hauling ore. Outside one village an old man sold boiled eggs and cupfuls of milk, and outside another a pig drover and his animals, caught in their cloud of dust, appeared like a spirit army on the horizon.

Mota had taken the Zacatecas route dozens of times. Lulled by its familiarity and by the easy tread of his horse, he let his mind open, caught and followed every memory, every thought: the morning his mother helped him dress for an interview with the priest to see if he had a vocation, the eight long days spent tracking a smuggler in the mist-swaddled mountains south of Oaxaca. He'd become so lost in memory's thicket that when, four days out of the city, Father Pascual began talking, Mota at first didn't notice.

"It is not one mine but several," Father Pascual was saying to the others, "that run along a single rich vein in a box canyon deep in the mountains."

Mota had pressed Father Pascual for details of Tayopa ever since they set out, but the man had refused to speak. All he knew were the rumors—that it lay beyond the farthest edge of Nueva Vizcaya, that the Jesuits who'd found it had worked it in secret so as not to pay the royal fifth, that the Indian uprising that had engulfed the northern provinces two years before had supposedly begun when the Jesuits' Yaqui slaves revolted. For years stories had circulated throughout New Spain, filigreed by each teller's imagination. That the Jesuits were building a grand desert city reached by flying boats was one of Mota's favorites, delivered from the tooth-scarce mouth of a coffee seller in Mérida as he trudged through the street beneath his urn.

"The country is empty and twisting," Father Pascual continued. "You could search for a dozen years and not find the mine. As much for secrecy as for fear of getting lost, no one was allowed to leave the canyon once he entered, except two of our brethren, who took the silver—only a fraction of it, mind you—to a mission near the coast, where it was packed in shipments of pilgrims' sandals bound for Rome.

"My third year at Tayopa I became attached to a youth of sixteen. I taught him our language, and when we were discovered we were punished. One night he and I escaped together. I planned to draw a map as we fled and sell it to the governor of Culiacán, to fund our new life. But my youth was killed by one of the Tepehuán guards who patrolled the outer paths. I had not been seen, and I ran in terror, blindly, through country I had crossed only once before. One month later the Yaquis rose and slaughtered the other Jesuits and the Tepehuáns. I hid in a mangrove swamp along the coast, getting provisions and news from a fishing camp of friendly Mayos, then made my way down to the city. Two years have passed since that Tepehuán guard took my happiness, two years during which I mourned and hid in fear of the Society, and I care for nothing now except that I get my pay and can flee this country."

For a few moments the five rode in silence. Then El Sepo spat. "He is a bugger. He admits it."

Mota looked at Father Pascual. He remembered the slender, dark-haired courtier's son who moved from bed to bed during his Salamanca days, thought of the rustlings he sometimes overheard in the camps. Such pleasures occurred, but one never spoke of them. "Are you?" Mota asked.

"I am," the ex-priest said. "And I suppose you could kill me." Here he paused, as if granting them the opportunity. "But then you wouldn't find the mine."

FIVE DAYS LATER they reached the shallow valley that was Zacatecas. The town lay sprawled below, spread before them like a felled giant, dormant in the late-afternoon sun. The mines, the camps, the stamping mills—all were silent, abandoned. In the refining yards, where normally teams of men stood in the quicksilvered sludge, chanting as they turned it with shovels, weeds now grew and piles of rusting tools awaited buyers. Mota had not visited Zacatecas in some time, but he had heard of its troubles. Two years ago the Crown had called in the miners' quicksilver debts, and immediately a third had gone bankrupt. Then four of the mines flooded, and not a month later came the worst calamity: the Santa María, the last of the rich mines, lost its vein.

Once they passed the emptied mining works they gained the town proper. Half the houses were shuttered, and those that weren't were flung open, flashing their gutted insides like a poor man presenting his turned-out pockets to a thief. Even the beggars had gone. And yet people still lived here: the thin smell of wood fire slipped through the air, and before the tread of their horses two dogs paused in the street, whined, and trotted on.

After a few hundred yards the Plaza de San Agustín opened before them, squared by four oak trees whose overburdened limbs knelt to the ground. Mota halted, the others pulling up behind him. The lodgings he had counted on were boarded up. As he contemplated the wide, blank wall of the convent that formed the plaza's west side—it, at least, was in good repair—he drank from his waterskin. Then, without an exchange of words, Mota guided the others up the next street, toward the Plaza Pública, where he remembered a tavern. They were halfway there when a man in a dusty velvet coat and dirt-stained shirt shot out in front of them from the large stone house on their right. The man waved his hands for them to stop. It took Mota several moments before he recognized him as Don Ignacio Peñafiel, the town's *alcalde*. Two years before he'd been fat, his lace cuffs like the traceries of powdered sugar decorating a pastry. Those lace cuffs, blackened with grime, now sagged from bony wrists.

"Don Juan," Don Ignacio said to Mota. "I almost don't believe my eyes. What brings you here?" The *alcalde* looked at the others, his jowls and neck loose with lost flesh. "You must be hungry, tired. Please, do me the honor of a visit. All your party are welcome to my home."

As soon as Mota accepted the offer, Don Ignacio turned and whistled, and two sour-faced Tepeque servants ambled from the house and guided the horses and mules into the courtyard. The animals stabled, Don Ignacio invited the white men to his second-floor parlor—Baltazar and El Sepo, Indian and mulatto, were to stay behind with the beasts—and begged them to sit while he busied himself at a broad, creaking credenza along the back wall, unlocking one of its cabinets with a key tied around his neck. Mota looked about the room. At first glance, it seemed in order, but on closer inspection he noted pale beards of dust hanging from the walls, holes in the curtains where insects had gnawed unchecked.

A pleased sigh emerged from the credenza, and, inching back out, Don Ignacio brought forth a half-emptied bottle of Madeira. After he stood he straightened his loose trousers and coat, then poured precise, small volumes of the wine into four glasses. He handed Mota the first.

"I hope you have not come to tax us more," Don Ignacio said.

"Don't worry," Mota answered. "My business is to the north."

"Is it?" Don Ignacio asked, then moved away to hand around the other glasses.

"Far to the north," Mota said. He sipped his Madeira. "But I confess," he added, "I never expected to find Zacatecas in such straits."

"Temporary, temporary," Don Ignacio said. "The vein will be found. The mines will be drained. The Crown will show mercy. I'm sure of it." He sat in the high-backed, spindle-legged chair he'd saved for himself, then looked at Mota, Fernando, and Father Pascual in turn. "Come now. I have heard a story. You are seeking Tayopa."

Mota shifted in his seat, turned his glass in his fingers. "It is just that," he said. "A story."

Don Ignacio grinned. "I've heard slabs of silver were left there, sitting out, waiting to be taken. I have two daughters in the convent. They send me tearstained letters. Their habits give them rashes.

They freeze at night and the nuns take away their blankets. One slab—just one slab—would see them married off."

Mota looked at the man. He remembered Don Ignacio's daughters, two egg-shaped creatures stuffed into silk. The last time he had visited, they had sat at the end of the room, large-eyed and silent as they snuck strips of ham from their handkerchiefs into their lapdogs' mouths. Then the *shatter-thump* of the stamping mills had resounded through the valley, reached even the *alcalde*'s curtained parlor, and Don Ignacio had been trying to distract him—with false protests and complaints—from the assay office accounts.

"The mine is fantasy," Mota said, and at this Don Ignacio remained silent until, some minutes later, a bell summoned them to a dinner of meatless stew.

Later that evening, past midnight, Mota woke to a rustling. He'd slept lightly, uncomfortable in Don Ignacio's house. Now, leaning his head up, he saw a figure crouched before his spilled packs: one of the Tepeques, turning papers over in the moonlight. Mota took his dagger from beneath his pillow and crept up to the Indian. Clapping one hand over the man's mouth, he brought the dagger point to his throat with the other. At the touch of steel, the Tepeque stiffened in his arms. Mota thought about pulling the dagger closer, feeling it slice into flesh, letting the Tepeque's blood stream over his fingers. He'd awoken clenched by a sorrow, and he hungered for whatever alchemy the Tepeque's blood might work in his heart. But instead, after holding him a little longer, he dragged the Indian to the door and with a kick set him free. Then he roused the others and within fifteen minutes they were riding out of town on the northern trail.

His brief time with María Isabel, Mota had long decided, had simply been an aberration from his life's regular, solitary course. While a boy in Seville, he'd often sat in the corner of his father's study, alone, and watched the other children in his quarter with a cold eye. They sometimes played beneath the study's window, and after they had left, in pursuit of some other pleasure, Mota would slip into the street to pick up the pig's bladder they had abandoned—he would blow into it, as they had, and marvel at how it stretched—or hide where the cleverest had hid during their last game. Sometimes the children found him and invited him to play. He would run with them as they made faces at the wandering Capuchin mendicant, stole a cone of sugar from the grocer's cart, halted with a hush before a bearded, iron-chested soldier on his mount. But always he felt a shadow between himself and those who were briefly his fellows.

The shadow had returned once María Isabel was put in the ground. During the years following Cuencamé, when Mota performed his work, assaying ores and checking ledgers, he shut himself away from others, and as his story was learned the people of the camps treated him with a careful respect, believing him to be in the grip of a melancholy that in time, as his injured heart healed, would be sloughed off. But he remained unchanged, and eventually their respect turned to disdain. They said he was like a spoiled child fed only on sweets, that he let pain rot within him. When Mota overheard this he agreed: he could feel the rot just beneath his skin, viscid and black.

IN DURANGO, cattle filled the streets, lowing and raising a dust that dimmed the sky while *vaqueros* circled and struck them with tasseled whips, readying them for the drive to the great mining camps at Parral. Two days beyond the town they crossed mud flats and wide salt marshes, then switchbacked up a rocky gap in the Sierra San Andrés. During the uprising, Father Pascual told them, a band of Conchos had set up in the gap and waylaid refugees from the coast. After the Conchos returned to the north, he'd heard, a presidio captain's daughter, a girl of thirteen, came out of the hills, belly round with child, tongue clipped from her mouth.

Six days later Mota and his men reached the ragged settlement that was Tamotchala, a single street of tents and half-finished adobe houses. In its fly-filled market Indians sat with vegetables and twists of rusted tin on their blankets, gathered from who knew where, while scrawny mules stood roped together, avoiding sale. It was a desperate, dreary place, but Mota, despite himself, felt a muffled fluttering in his gut. He had been to Tamotchala just once before, to inspect the nearby Ojo de Dios mine, a pit worked by a handful of creoles and half bloods living beneath stick shelters. But he'd never been beyond the town. Few had. Above Tamotchala spread the blank parchment of the viceroy's map.

A SANDY INDIAN TRACK LED NORTH and cut through a forest of dry, tangled trees choked with cactus. Mota and the others picked it up just across the river from Tamotchala and for days followed it without event. They passed two abandoned settlers' clearings, cabins burned and corrals torn down during the uprising, and after the fourth stream they crossed they came upon patches of tilled bean fields, a village of dried mud, and a square of ash and blackened timber. Indians in the fields and in the mud houses stopped their work and looked.

"These are the Mayos," Father Pascual whispered in Mota's ear. "That"—he nodded discreetly at the ashen square—"was one of our missions."

The Mayos watched as Mota and the others passed through. It seemed to satisfy the Indians that the party wasn't stopping but continuing on. Over the next days the forest began to thin. Their third day from the village, they rode past bleached bones, and the sixth day out they arrived at the grassy edge of a wide river. Mota saw a mud break in the distant reeds, the track continuing on the river's other side. But before he could ford the river, Father Pascual stopped him. They had entered Yaqui territory, and this was the water they must follow east.

"First to the village of Bacom," Father Pascual said, "and from there to Cocorim, and then into the mountains."

Cottonwoods grew along the river, but soon gave way to another bean field, at the end of which was a village much like that of the Mayos, with mud houses and a few old stilt huts of mat and cane. As they approached the village, Father Pascual hung at the back. Since leaving Mexico, he had grown out his beard, and now he pressed his hat low on his head.

Just as in the Mayo village, they were watched from hut and field, but here an old man in a long cotton shirt waited for them in the middle of the track. He didn't move as Mota approached, and when Mota halted the old man asked their business in piecemeal Spanish.

"We're riding into the mountains," Mota said. He had worried there might be trouble when they reached this part of the journey. It was from here, the country along the river, the Jesuits had taken their slaves. But the soldiers had been cruel when they came north to put down the rebellion, and Mota hoped the memory of that cruelty would be fresh in the Yaquis' minds, make them wary and timid. He listened to the dull slide of metal against leather, El Sepo drawing his ivory-handled stiletto.

The old Yaqui spat. "Nothing good in the mountains."

"We go under orders of the king. We have no dealings with the Jesuits."

"Mountains empty," the old Yaqui said. "You turn back." He watched Mota with flinty eyes, but when Mota spurred his horse, the man got out of his way.

Messengers must have sprinted through the bean fields with whispers of their arrival, for in the next village—the one called Cocorim—Yaquis lined the path. No one tried to stop Mota or the others, but one Yaqui danced before them as they rode, contorting to show the curdled skin of his burnt shoulder, the ridged lash marks along his back, his broken, twisted arm. He yelped and turned, and as Mota watched him turn again he saw the vacancy in his rolling eyes, the absence of a reason long since lost.

AFTER MARÍA ISABEL, Mota had made formal court to no other woman. At times on his journeys daughters were presented to him like goods at auction; he would politely confess their charms and keep a committed bachelor's distance. Beyond the occasional camp woman and the more common stretches of solitude, he'd confined his desires to the widowed sister of the baker from whom he rented his room in Mexico, and the skinny, untended wife of a Pueblo horse dealer, who preferred to meet him in the stable and wear a blindfold while he took her from behind. Like the beasts, she insisted—she would have it no other way. But in the last year the baker's widowed sister had cut off their liaison, as she was being courted in earnest by a pastry maker, and the horse dealer's wife had suddenly turned pious, pretending not to know him the last two times he had visited. Without their comforts, he'd felt the rot spread through him unchecked. New Spain, that great mill to which the unhappy and disappointed of the world came to be stamped anew, had left him ever as he was.

Then the viceroy had spoken the name Tayopa, and Mota's heart had beaten briefly within his chest. He cursed himself as a fool, but such discoveries had transformed other men. He often saw them racing their pasteled carriages through the streets of Mexico, laughter and feminine squeals escaping from their windows.

WITHIN TWO DAYS they were beyond Yaqui lands. Now the river bent, flowing from the north, and they kept alongside it, riding into craggy foothills grown with sparse stands of oak and pine. Mountain Indians—Opata—were said to live here, but there was no trace of them, and blended in with the regular tick of nature's chatter there seemed a particular silence.

After another day's ride they passed through a scattering of abandoned stone huts, and four days later they came to a bottleneck too narrow to lead their mounts through. Without speaking they backtracked, and when Mota spotted an animal path they walked the horses and mules up it until they reached a small plateau, which gave onto a new canyon. They halted there while Fernando penciled their trail and El Sepo looked through the spyglass. Mota took a piece of biscuit from his pack. He was picking out weevils with the point of his knife when he heard El Sepo whisper, "Cattle."

Putting the biscuit in his pocket, Mota took the spyglass from El Sepo and looked where he pointed. In the canyon below, four mottled cows stood in a clump of dried grass. Their ribs showed through their hides; they looked lost, half-wild, and Mota wondered how they had gotten here. Then he moved the spyglass, and the air caught in his lungs. On a rock, watching over the cattle, sat a woman. Long hair hung loose over her back. Mota goaded his horse over to Father Pascual.

"I thought this country was empty," he said, keeping his voice low.

THEY RODE DOWN. Their path took them through several knots of pine, blocking their view of the woman's rock, and when they reached the bottom of the canyon she was gone.

Mota sent El Sepo to track the woman while he and the others waited by the stream. Perhaps they should ignore her and travel on, but he'd seen through the glass that she wasn't an Indian and he was curious. Besides, she might know something of the mine.

When El Sepo returned, he reported that the woman was hiding in a cave. He told too of a hut farther up the canyon—likely the woman's—and Mota sent the others there to wait. Meanwhile he followed El Sepo up a path and then a ledge into a blind hollow high above the canyon. Here the cave opened atop a slope of red dirt. Mota motioned for El Sepo to stay where he was while he climbed. A few feet from the cave's mouth, he stopped. The sun was directly above, and no light fell into the cave's interior. "Don't be frightened," Mota shouted. "We only want to talk to you. We've come from Mexico. We can take you there, or to any town on our path."

There was no answer. Mota looked down at El Sepo. El Sepo shrugged.

"I'm coming inside," Mota said to the cave, and stepped in.

Beyond the first, penumbral feet, the cave's void was entire. Mota fumbled over a blind jag of rocks, then stopped and listened. Silence. She was there, somewhere before him, behind the darkness. He strained his eyes, willed them to adjust. They refused, flooded black, liquid and numb. Mota moved forward, then stopped again when he heard the scrape of bare feet.

In an instant she was on him, a tangle of limbs pulling him down, and just as quickly he felt a sudden, sharp pain in his side. He caught her by the waist, held her squirming body to him. She struggled, but he kept her close and pulled her toward the sun. Once they were out of the cave she clawed at him, grunted and screamed, and El Sepo rushed up and took her by the arms. She kicked and stomped, but the mulatto carried her down the slope with ease. Free of the woman, Mota inspected his side. She'd stuck him with a cactus needle. He removed it—it slid easily from his flesh, drawing a bubble of blood—and dropped it among the brambles.

A DIFFERENT PATH LED OUT OF THE HOLLOW, and as they took it the woman traded her kicking for hanging lifeless against El Sepo's grip, dragging her feet into a stumble. Still, she barely slowed them, and when they arrived at the hut Mota whistled at Father Pascual and gestured for him and Fernando to join them inside. El Sepo had already taken the woman there, and Mota could hear her shouting. As they entered she turned and made her address general. "Go ahead. Rape me. See how you like it. I'm stuffed with glass and quills."

The woman sat on a rickety stool and El Sepo stood over her, his arms crossed. Her brown skin was reddened from the sun, and her body was animal-lean save for the loose breasts that swung beneath her shift as she twisted toward each of them. She might be a quarter blood, but Mota wasn't sure.

"Please," the woman said. "It would be such pleasure."

"Enough!" Mota said. "None of us will harm you."

This quieted the woman, though she continued to tremble.

"Just a few questions and we will leave you, if that's what you wish," he said. "We're looking for a mine. Do you know anything about a mine?"

"When the Yaquis came, hammers and picks in their hands, I learned."

"Have you been to it?"

"No."

"Do you know where it is?"

"No."

Mota glanced about the ramshackle cabin. It was little over three *varas* on either side. Dried plants and a pair of rust-bitten pots hung from the ceiling. On the far side of the room slumped a narrow bed. Maize leaves and feathers wriggled from its split mattress.

"How long have you been here on your own?"

"I'm not on my own."

Mota laughed at the thinness of her lie. "How long?"

She looked away. "Two years," she said.

Before Mota finished questioning the woman, he learned her name was Beatriz and that she had been married at fifteen to a rancher named Tómas, who had brought her here and been killed by the Yaquis—an event over which she showed little regret. She had nothing else to tell them and after they bartered with her for a string of dried sausages they rode away from her hut. Mota had offered again to take her with them, but she'd only stared at him. That night they made camp near the top of a ridge. As Mota was talking to Fernando and examining the maps, he spotted Father Pascual with the sackcloth bag he'd had the morning they left Mexico. Throughout their journey it had remained hidden. Mota watched as Father Pascual unknotted the bag then stuck his hand inside and pulled out a bull's horn. Fernando made to get up, but Mota reached out to stop him. Holding the horn, Father Pascual scrambled to the top of the ridge, and, once he'd steadied himself, blew. The blast shot across the dusk, echoed against the slope that faced their camp, then fell away.

Father Pascual blew the horn again. After the last echo, again from the slope, he came back.

Mota was baffled. When he asked Father Pascual what he was doing, the ex-Jesuit said he was listening for Tayopa. Mota felt a flash of sickness—they'd come all this way with a madman. He ordered Father Pascual to explain himself. "There's a particular echo," the man said. "One of the mountain Indians, who led Father Xavier to the mine, told him of it. Once we left the woman's canyon, I could tell we were near. When you hear the echo, you've found the valley."

"What does it sound like?" Mota asked, the sickness gone, replaced instead by something rarer, something like wonder.

The sackcloth bundle returned to the pack, Father Pascual pulled out his bedroll. "No, no," he said. "I tell you, and then what am I worth? I don't think so. I am not in the mood to have my throat slit."

FOR THE NEXT THREE DAYS they continued east while Father Pascual climbed every slope and promontory and blew his horn. Mota's fascination quickly dulled, and in the length of these days his mind refused to wander. He monitored the dry passages of his bowels, thought of the slight, pinkish mound that remained on the side of his belly, where he had been stuck with the cactus needle. At times it throbbed and he touched it. Pressing it made the throb sharpen then disappear.

He'd been fingering the needle wound when he was thrown by his horse. As they were riding across a gully, the horse stepped on a rattlesnake. Bit, it reared, and Mota landed in the gully's creekbed, his leg catching against a rock. For a moment he lay dazed, trapped still in his thoughts, thinking the fall had happened there. Then a sharp pain streaked up his leg.

The others were shouting, and as Mota tried to sit up El Sepo pinned his shoulders. Baltazar's impassive face, a frowning moon, hovered above him. He was their bonesetter, and as he felt along the leg, a new, dizzying pain cut through Mota's flesh.

"Is it bad?" Fernando asked.

"An even break," Baltazar answered. "It could be worse."

Mota ignored the pain as he listened. He wanted to apologize, but was too ashamed to speak. Had he not been distracted, he might have checked his horse or at least landed better. The last thing they needed was yet more delay. He stared up at the sky, blue, distant; at the gnarled finger of an oak where a jay chirped and twitched its head. He counted days on his fingers. Tamotchala, the nearest town, was over two weeks away, and it was half lean-tos and tents. Mota tried sitting up again. He wanted to stand on his leg, to punish it, to let the pain surge through it, but El Sepo kept his hold on his shoulders. All the while his horse snorted in mad bursts. Its tackle jangled as it shifted and danced. It thought it could cast off the snakebite, but it was mistaken. It would have to be killed.

Baltazar, who'd left, now returned with branches and rope. He knelt over Mota and worked the bone, twisting and pushing it into place: Mota bit and groaned as the pain flashed then settled then flashed again. Above him was the sky's clean blue, the undisturbed jay. At last the bone was set, and Mota lay there a moment, sweat dripping from his skin, then said, "The search is everything. Leave me with provisions and a pistol."

"Don't be foolish," El Sepo said. "We can make our camp here."

"This is already slow work," Mota said, then jerked his head at Father Pascual. "He has to blow that cursed horn forty times a day. If you stay here, it'll slow the search even more."

"But we can't just leave you," Fernando said.

"I agree," Baltazar said. "Besides, you need shelter."

"Take him to the woman's hut," offered Father Pascual, who'd been silent the entire time. "It's not far."

At this the others paused. Their search had been slow, and they could make the hut by nightfall. Fernando and Baltazar quickly took up the idea, and as they talked Mota remembered the feel of the woman—beating, warm—as he'd dragged her from the cave. Since they'd left her, the image of her feral body in its thin shift had pulled on his mind.

WHEN THEY ARRIVED AT THE HUT, at dusk, the woman was not to be found. Mota was not surprised. He had assumed she would startle at the first noise of their coming. The others carried him from the mule they had balanced him on to the bed, then brought in his pack and a pair of crutches Baltazar had fashioned. They sat with him for an hour and played cards. Mota thought he should say something, but he'd never encouraged intimacy, rarely inquired of his companions' lives beyond the trail. El Sepo suggested, for the third time, that either he or Fernando stay with him, but Mota shook his head. "The mine," he said.

In the morning, the woman still hadn't appeared, and at this Mota felt a pinprick of sorrow. Father Pascual was already on his mule when El Sepo and Fernando took their leave, standing over him awkwardly, and Baltazar gave the leg a final inspection. Then they put on their hats and left, and Mota was alone, the wooden hut empty save for a pair of flies that traced a crooked path above him.

The hours crawled alongside the doorway's shifting portion of sun. Maize leaves poked through the mattress and gave him sweat rashes. Mota stood only to piss and defecate into a bowl. Baltazar had cautioned him against using the crutches overmuch in the first days, and, his leg still throbbing, it was all Mota could do to make it to the door and scatter his waste.

A WEEK PASSED, a long, slow week. The woman never came to the hut, but, after the first days Baltazar had warned him of, Mota began hobbling around the clearing outside, then wandering farther up the canyon, working the crutches over roots and stone. His third day out he found her. As before, she was with the cattle. They stood in a rocky clearing, and she sat in the shade of a knobbly pine.

"Hello," he called.

"You are walking," she answered without looking up.

He hobbled closer, saw that a small red carcass lay at her side. Before her was spread the animal's skin.

"I am," he said. Though he hadn't admitted it to himself, in his wandering he'd been looking for her. He thought to get nearer, but stopped himself, lest he rewake the mad fright she'd displayed when he pulled her from the cave. "I'm sorry to have forced you from your bed," he added.

"It is no matter," she said. She scraped at the skin.

"I'd be pleased if you returned," he said. "I promise you, I am harmless. As you see, I'm slowed." He tapped his leg and grinned. "I have books with me. Reports from Mexico. I could read to you, if you like. Surely, after so much time alone, you want for companionship."

Her eyes remained down, on the skin, as if she did not hear him. But Mota knew something in her was curious. Otherwise she would have fled before he appeared, as she had done when he and the others had first ridden down toward her rock.

"Or poems—I have pamphlets left with me by one of my men. Winners from the city's last competition and other such things."

She hesitated in her scraping, then picked up the skin and, without meeting Mota's eyes, retreated beyond the pine tree and into a clump of others. Mota's leg ached from standing, and so with an unanswered farewell he pivoted on his good leg and swung himself back toward the cabin.

THE NEXT MORNING he went looking for Beatriz, but she did not allow herself to be found. The curiosity he had detected had been pure illusion, he decided, the sad imagining of a withered heart. But in the night that followed he was woken by breath on his face, an elbow sharply pinching his chest. His eyes opened to darkness, and in that first terror he flung out a hand. It struck a shoulder, ribs, the curve of a back. Beneath his palm flesh stretched against bone, surprisingly smooth. Fingers wrestled with his trousers and he helped, pushed the trousers down. The night phantom was astride him now, and, his leg stiff and awkward in its splint, the creaking bed's maize leaves poking his back, they coupled, the woman's grunting nothing like María Isabel's dutiful cries. She held him at the shoulders, either to anchor herself or keep him pinned, and he bit his lips shut for fear of frightening her away. She groaned when he loosed himself, then waited for him to lengthen again.

The next morning Beatriz was still there, asleep and curled against him. With care he negotiated his way over her and out of the bed, then went to the door and cleared his bladder. When he turned around she was sitting up, yawning with arms stretched, and he tried to decide if she was beautiful. "Read me some of those things you brought from the city," she said when she finished her yawn. He grabbed the satchel of books and went to the bed. Whenever he stopped, pausing after a *mascarada* song or an account of a sea battle with the English—all the stuff and trash of life for which he had no taste—she said, More, more. She dug herself into him with her backside, pulled his arm over her, and he indulged a fantasy of taking her back to Mexico, presenting her to the viceroy as a marvel, a wild woman tamed. He would live with her in a fine palace bought with his earnings from the mine; though dressed in silk, she would keep her wildness and bear him a string of cubs. Others would speak of him as the man who had found Tayopa in the wastes, who had rescued a near savage from the lands beyond the frontier, and he would be changed—no longer the man who had let ten years silt away into nothing, the man who had buried himself in a lead coffin and joined himself with the dead. His mouth tired of so much reading and he begged a respite. Beatriz said she would allow it, and as he lay back she told him scraps of her life: that her mother sold her for a year's worth of meat, that she had begged her husband not to take her from their village outside Querétaro, that he had beaten her when the midwife pulled a daughter, stillborn, from her. They had been lured here by the Jesuits, she said, who had told them they were supplying missions in the far north and forbade them to leave their ranch. She had hidden in her cave when the Yaquis had come, had refused to weep when she found her husband and the other ranchers slaughtered. As she spoke she shifted at random to whispers, covered her eyes, made crosses on Mota's arm—traces of the small but important something in her that had long been rattled loose. After, she fed him a mash of corn and dried meat. When he mentioned the city to her, said he wanted to take her there, she answered that she wanted to go.

Two days later, they heard the shuffling hoofbeats of a horse in trot. Mota was in the bed, resting his leg, and Beatriz was lying beside him. She startled, and he held her. The hoofbeats drew closer, and soon after they stopped Fernando appeared in the doorway and looked down at them. "We've found it," he said.

FERNANDO HAD GRINNED AT THE WOMAN, and at Mota's insistence they bring her with them. Such a demand, Mota knew, was much unlike the self he had long presented his fellows. But Fernando quickly swept the grin away and said, "Of course."

When they left, Mota and Beatriz sat atop Fernando's horse while Fernando walked it and told Mota of the mine. It was a three days' ride away, he said, and they hadn't actually seen it—as soon as Father Pascual identified the canyon they'd turned around, believing Mota, as inspector, should be with them. But the ex-Jesuit assured him there could be no doubt. He'd recognized the country, and the horn's echo was unmistakable.

The others were waiting for Mota at a camp not far from the canyon. They betrayed the same muted astonishment at the woman's presence as Fernando had, but otherwise kept their distance from her and avoided her gaze, as if fearing she might be ill luck. Once Mota was helped off the horse Baltazar poked his fingers inside the splint. "Better," he pronounced. "But it'll need at least six more weeks." Meanwhile, El Sepo launched into his own version of how they found the mine, telling how he had danced a quick jig and Father Pascual had refused to smile. Mota seemed to miss every other word. Night had fallen, and on the far side of the fire, where its light bled into darkness, Beatriz was bedding down, away from them. The distance ached. When El Sepo finished his story, Baltazar leaned over to Mota and said, "I bet she was hungry for it, she ride you cross-eyed?"

Two days later they came to a shelf of rock beneath which the country flattened. Mota and Beatriz had shared a mule, she mounted in front of him as he kept his hands on the reins, his arms around her. The country from atop the shelf of rock looked no different from anywhere else they'd ridden through, but here they stopped and Father Pascual took his horn from his pack and blew. The first echo was faint, but the second came back louder than the original blast.

"Tayopa," Father Pascual said, pointing to a break in the valley's far side. The last echo had come from there.

They crossed the valley, halting at a stream that purled out of the break, which, Mota saw now, was the mouth of a narrow *ba-rranca*. Alongside the stream led a trail covered with broken shale, disappearing as it bent. A breeze coursed out of the *barranca*'s mouth, fluttered over Mota's face. In front of him Beatriz shifted as she cursed the mule's backbone. They rode in.

After forty *varas* a red shoulder of rock forced path and stream into a tight embrace, and once they eased around the shoulder they came to a round, two-story building.

"The first guardhouse," Father Pascual said.

Past the guardhouse the trail and the stream twisted north. The walls of rock began to widen, and the bunchgrass and the *madroños,* which had granted the narrow path a dappled green light, started to thin, giving way to ropy thornbushes. Then the trail swiftly mounted several layers of rock, and Mota and the others found themselves in the wide, barren bowl of a box canyon— Tayopa. In the middle of the bowl, attached to the roofless skeleton of a church, stood a bell tower, its sides licked with soot. Machinery from a smelting works lay broken and half-buried, and patterns of mud and stone rubble were scattered between the bell tower and a circle of kilns. Beyond loomed the dark piles of slag, and all around, in the basin's walls, watched the black, hollowed eyes that were the entrances to the mines.

Mota tightened his grip on Beatriz—she had shuddered, at what he wasn't sure—and took in the brown and red slope of the far ridge. The air smelled of dried, flaking dirt, and the wind coming over the ridge carried an empty sound. Mota closed his ears to it, buried his nose in Beatriz's matted hair, erected once more in his mind the vision of their return. But this did nothing to still the shadow that had stirred once more in his heart.

With the aid of his crutch, he slipped down from the mule. They would be weeks, assaying samples from the mines and the slag heaps, logging troves, scouting new routes from the mine. The sooner they started, the sooner they could leave.

AMY

I HAD BEEN IN WIESBADEN FOR TWO WEEKS. This was in October 2009. The German semester hadn't started yet, and so neither had my job, and after a first week surrendered to various bureaucracies I was spending a chain of sunny days exploring. On the third such day, after taking the little yellow funicular up the Neroberg and hiking down, I was walking in the pedestrian-zoned city center and had paused to look through the window of the gummy candy store. Thoughts of a present shipped home to my nephews took breath then perished (the postage, the hassle) before somebody behind me said, "Holy shit," and grabbed me by the arm.

The words with their three flat American syllables leapt at me from the German public's constant guttural hum. I turned and a short, nicely thick-bodied woman with light green eyes and rusted blond hair was looking up at me, mouth hanging open in a display of shock. My memory fumbled, then immediately I had a flash of her at fifteen: studded leather choker around her neck, bottle of cherry soda constantly stowed in her backpack, Mod Podged collages of ads from *Spin* magazine covering her folders. Amy Heathcock. She'd been two years behind me in high school, and we'd been members of separate outcast cliques that shared the hallway outside the band room for standing around in the mornings before class. Once we'd gone on a date, and later, when I was home from college, I ran into her at the Corny Dog in the Longview Mall, where she dipped hot dogs in batter. But by the time she clutched my arm in Langgasse I'd forgotten she existed.

"What are you doing here?" she said. She smiled and freed her other hand from a stroller to pull me into a hug.

"I'm teaching," I said, neglecting to mention I was also fleeing a failing marriage—arguably the truer answer. "What about you?"

"I'm staying with a friend," she said. The friend's husband was army, she explained, stationed at the airfield outside town, and they lived in one of the blocks of married housing on the other side of the train station. I nodded. The day before I'd taken a bus in that direction and seen a Popeye's and a Taco Bell locked behind a tall, guarded fence. "This is my Macy," Amy added, looking down at the two-year-old who lay in the stroller's seat, passed out. "She likes it when I push her through here. Sometimes it's all I can do to get her to sleep." Amy looked up again. In that moment she seemed barely changed in the decade-plus from the girl I remembered. The same freckled nose with its mousy tip, the same sly light in her eyes, the same thin T-shirt fabric pulling across the same soft pouch of belly. She said we should hang out and I agreed.

WE WENT TO THE CAFÉ MALDANER, just around the corner, where we picked slices of cake from a glass case and sat in the high-ceilinged, wood-paneled tearoom. I'd wanted to go inside the Maldaner since I first saw it. According to the gold lettering on the window, it dated to 1859, and I imagined Dostoevsky, who'd lived here in the 1860s, drinking coffee inside as he fretted about the previous evening's losses at the gaming tables.

As we sat Amy tended to her daughter. She had woken, and, after staring silently at me for three minutes ("Macy, this is one of Mommy's friends," Amy had said), she started throwing her toys at a mink-coated frau whose spun-sugar sphere of white hair made an irresistible target. The toys kept landing short, and I would pick them up and give them to Amy, who would give them back to the crying Macy, who would throw them again. I wondered if this was all that would happen and if it was for the best. But after Macy's

fit, as Amy asked me about high school—who I still saw, if I remembered this or that drama—she took my hand, and once we
finished our cake I walked her to my apartment. There we parked
Macy in front of the TV, which I turned to KiKA, the children's
channel, and we went into the bedroom. As we stood together,
Amy's back pressed against me, I lifted her skirt and bit her neck.
She squealed—I remembered that squeal, heard sometimes in the
hallway before class whenever another sex-deprived, aching boy
poked or tickled her generous flesh. Then she told me to hurry. We
only had until the cartoon ended.

AFTER WE FINISHED she wheeled Macy out of my apartment, and
I sat down to work on my syllabi. I'd given Amy my phone number and my e-mail address, but as I looked at my laptop's screen I
hoped that was it, that she would step back into her life and I into
mine. The last thing I wanted was a new entanglement.

So when she called me a few days later, asking if I'd like to meet
her, I was worried.

"Just for an hour," she said.

"My wife," I said.

"You said you haven't talked to her in a month."

"Macy."

"I'll leave her with Beth."

She waited while I said nothing. I found myself thinking of the
large, milk-white breasts that I'd admired at sixteen and that, as
we'd stood in my bedroom, had remained bound behind her bra,
unexplored.

"I'm not sure," I said.

"Think of it this way. We're friends. What's wrong with being
friends?"

But we'd never been friends. She was just a girl I'd happened to
know years ago. Still, it was enough. Two hours later I was waiting for her outside the Karstadt, one of the massive, glass-walled

shopping centers downtown. She showed wearing jeans and hoop earrings, and I felt twelve years younger, the entirety of my life spread before me, unmade.

MY WIFE SAT enshrined chief among the mistakes and disappointments I'd come to Germany to escape. I met her in my third year at Michigan, when she was a first-year fresh from a small liberal arts college in Maine. Clara came from an old-money family of Chicago lawyers, bred for summers at Saugatuck and seats on museum boards, and attended our graduate seminars in peasant dresses no peasant could afford and high leather boots that pressed smoothly against her calves. At parties she would stand in the corner telling practiced stories to a small, rapt circle of fellow students clutching bottles of Oberon or Winter White. About the night the president (before he was president) came for cocktails: "He had really hairy ears. You think someone would tell him." About the year after her parents' divorce: "I met my dad each week at this Chinese place. I always ordered the Happy Family." A pause, then a half smile. "He never got the joke."

That I made her love me, that I somehow entered her existence and found a place in it—the comfiest chair in the living room of her soul—I still count as the greatest accomplishment of my reinvention. I had been a sweaty, acned nobody from a small town in East Texas that most people had never heard of, then a scholarship student at the state university with no claim on anything higher than the dreary futures (pharmaceutical sales, a chain store's management track) touted at the job fairs held each year in our basketball arena. But a marathon semester spent polishing an application essay ended with me in a grad program where my peers were people with the kinds of East Coast, private-school educations I had long envied. By the time I met Clara I had transformed myself, through the alchemy of a research assistantship with a famous theorist and a paper on Spinoza and Coleridge given at a major conference, into a promising scholar, a rising star of the department. I was climbing, never so sure of what I was climbing toward until I saw Clara standing in her circle—her hair loose over her temples, her upper lip pooched by the slightest of overbites—exuding class privilege like a musk.

We married a year later. The ceremony was small, in the chapel of a large downtown Chicago church, St. James Episcopal. The other graduate students dubbed us the power couple, and we took an apartment in a house in the Old West Side with a porch we'd sit on when it was warm, drinking gin and tonics, and two spare rooms we used as offices. Clara dressed me in thrift store blazers, idly ran her fingers through my thinning hair while she read. In the summer we spent long weeks at her family's place on Lake Michigan, swimming and working through stacks of books. Our happiness seemed unquestionable. But the following spring, after a semester spent trying to break ground on my dissertation—"Representations of Eastern Europeans in the Nineteenth-Century Novel," chosen after a misleadingly exuberant seminar—I had a crisis. I saw all my future years spent waking to wrestle with murky thoughts, to put cold words on cold pages no one would ever read. It was a rather mundane crisis, my adviser told me, but I didn't get over it. Meanwhile, Clara had turned into a plodding worker, in her office every morning, and only now that we were married did I discover that what I'd thought was a quiet, aristocratic disdain was instead pure shyness, that her affected coolness shrouded a sentimental heart. I had expected the air in this new world to which I'd laid claim to be different, to ease me past imperfection and strife in a narcotic mist. But sealed together in that house, Clara and I began to fight. Usually I was the provoker, coming to Clara with some correction I thought she could make to her habits or person (the dissertation abandoned, I had little else to brood about). At first, whenever I caught the sound of her crying behind her office door, I'd go to her, apologize, but eventually I chose to leave her be and waited instead for her to come to dinner, amnesic smile pinned to her face. When, at the end of summer, I told her about the job in Germany, a one-year exchange appointment I'd begged from our grad director, she said she didn't want me to go, but within a day she'd packed my things in a box.

AMY AND I BEGAN MEETING on Mondays and Fridays. I taught the other days of the week at the university in Mainz, and the weekends, I told her, I needed for grading, though in fact I simply wanted to keep them to myself. Sometimes we took trips: In Bad Homburg we strolled through the Kurpark with its Thai temples and miniature Russian church, then toured the kaiser's summer palace where the guide showed us first the kaiser's telephone cabinet, with its private line to Berlin, then the kaiser's flush toilet, with its view over the palace roof. In Höchst we wandered into the toll castle's moat, a green, ivy-strewn park abandoned that day under a gray sky, and in Rüdesheim we sat on a rock in a muddy, bare vineyard, getting drunk on grape brandy while we watched the Rhine flow by, its long, thin cargo barges easing their way to Rotterdam. On our trips I found it difficult to contain myself. In the vineyard I brought her head to my lap and unzipped my jeans as hikers passed a hundred feet above us, and in the Höchst moat I'd leaned her into a corner and slipped my fingers inside her waistband before a man overhead whistled, his head poking out from the castle's high tower, which cost a euro to climb.

The days we didn't take trips we spent in my apartment, and the days we did take trips we always ended there. As soon as we closed the door we'd shed our clothes and scurry to bed, me getting up and dressing only to fetch our dinner from the dimly lit takeaway—Indian food, pizza, schnitzels—four doors down. We never talked of our lives beyond the age of nineteen, only of prom, football games, and the bored, unending nights spent driving the

Longview loop. One afternoon she went through the catalog of girls we'd known, asking which ones I'd had crushes on, and giggled anytime I said yes and for at least two declared, "Skank!" Another time I brought up our date.

She blushed. "I was wondering when you'd ask about that."

"So you do remember?"

She looked at me. "What about you? What do you remember?"

"You barely spoke to me. I took you to the Jalapeño Tree and we ate fajitas, then I asked you what you wanted to do and somehow we ended up at a soccer game. We sat in my car and all I wanted to do the whole time was feel you up, but I could tell you just wanted to go home."

"I was horrible!" she said. "I was really into you when you asked me out, but by the end of the week I wasn't. I was like that all sophomore year." Then she kicked back the sheets and sat atop me, leaning down so that her breasts pressed against my chest. "Have I made up for it now?"

I admitted she had.

Since arriving in Wiesbaden, I'd been trying, off and on, to find out where Dostoevsky had lived during his time in the city. I'd had no luck (even Google had turned up nothing) until early in November I spent an afternoon hiking on the Neroberg. At the Russian cemetery I happened upon a faded display, in Russian and German, recording the history of Russian notables in the area, and next to Dostoevsky's name I saw Hotel Viktoria.

I was going to wait until Saturday to look for the hotel, but Amy said she wanted to come with me. As we were walking together down Wilhelmstrasse, the street where most of the old spa hotels had stood, she asked me why I wanted to find where Dostoevsky stayed. The truth was I hadn't read him since college. But he'd lived in Wiesbaden, and now I did: there was hope in the parallel, depth I could glom on to. If nothing else, the search for his hotel would be a good detail to drop over drinks in Ann Arbor. Before I could make up some different, better answer, though, Amy took my hand in hers and swung it a little and said, "If you wrote something, what would you write about me?"

I thought for a moment. We passed the Meissen shop, its porcelain goat staring mutely through the window, and then I said, "That you had nice thighs and you helped me through a bad time."

The question had been asked in a jokey tone, and I had answered in a jokey tone, but at my reply she grew quiet.

After we walked another block she slipped her hand from mine.

"I'm sorry," I said. "I'm not sure what you wanted me to say."

"Nothing," she said. "I was just being stupid." When I glanced at her she smiled. I was practiced at detecting false smiles, but I was practiced at ignoring them, too.

I'd asked about the old Hotel Viktoria in the tourist office, and the woman behind the counter had first consulted a book and then made a phone call before telling me that it stood on the northeast corner of Wilhelmstrasse and Rheinstrasse. We arrived there and I stopped and looked up. The Viktoria was dressed in red stone and had curving, wrought-iron balconies. It wasn't a hotel anymore but offices, its bottom floors given over to an interior design firm and a shop selling ballet clothes. In the summer of 1865 Dostoevsky had holed up here and feverishly churned out his first draft of *Crime and Punishment*. Judging by the names on the plate next to the main door, his room belonged now to either a notary or a foot doctor. I'd expected to feel something, for inspiration to zap out from the stones and grip me, but it was just a building.

Later, as we lay in bed, bellies full of chicken korma from down the street, Amy's head resting on my chest, she said, "I like you."

Since our conversation on Wilhelmstrasse, things had been unsettled between us. "I like being with you, okay?"

"Okay," I said. "I like being with you, too."

A FEW DAYS LATER, Clara called. It was a Thursday and I'd spent the day teaching and had had to keep reminding myself that it was actually Thanksgiving. Clara and I hadn't talked in two months, and after she wished me Happy Thanksgiving we didn't say much else until she asked, "Are you flying home for Christmas?"

"I'm not sure," I said.

"Do you want to fly back?"

I didn't say anything.

"I need to know what to tell my parents."

"I know," I said.

"Well, what should I tell them?"

There was the slightest quaver in her voice. I couldn't hear the murmur of family behind her. She must have been up in her room, sitting on her bed, the door shut. In my mind I saw her there, the lights turned off and light coming in from the street, her face pointed toward the stable of horse figurines from her girlhood. Through the deadness of my heart I felt a throb.

"Well?" she said again.

I told her, "I'm not sure," and she hung up.

THE PHONE CALL was still troubling me when, a day later, Amy and I were sitting in bed. It was rainy and cold and we'd stayed in. Pulling closer to me, Amy told me that she and Macy were going to Rothenburg with Beth and her husband next week and she wanted me to come with them.

"Seriously?" I said.

"It'll be fun."

I tried to picture the five of us on a jaunt together. I couldn't.

"No, I don't think so," I said, and added something about grading.

She put a leg on top of mine, rested her chin on my chest, and looked at me. She was smiling, but I didn't know how long I had. "Fine," I said. "Okay. Yes."

THE FOLLOWING FRIDAY, the day set for the trip, a beat-up red Opel honked for me at nine. Amy introduced me to Beth and then Wesley, whom I gave a shy glance. His face was red and pitted and his upper lip bore a sparse brown mustache. We'd been at war for eight years and I hadn't yet talked to a soldier. I was assigned the passenger seat, and Amy and Beth sat together in the back, Macy buckled into her car seat directly behind me.

As Wesley guided us out of town he didn't speak, but once we were on the highway he started talking. He drifted from the trips he and Beth had taken to Cologne and Neuschwanstein to karaoke at the Irish Pub to run-ins between his fellow soldiers and the polizei—one soldier caught flying up the autobahn, drunk, throwing beer bottles at the cars coming the other direction, another found passed out in his car, four in the morning, beneath a traffic light deep in the Wiesbaden suburbs. "Don't fuck with the polizei," he warned me. "They'll fine your ass." I waited for an opportune moment to mention my father's combat in Vietnam. Those rare times I felt guilt over not going to war in this our decade of troubles, he was my excuse. He did that, so I didn't have to—he'd actually said that to me once. But Wesley didn't bring up Iraq or Afghanistan, though Amy told me he'd been to both, and at the end of each of his stories I simply smiled and laughed politely.

We arrived at Rothenburg and found the place already filled with tourists, half of them American: I spotted their SUVs in the parking lot, imported Explorers and Escalades with Frankfurt or Munich plates, the owners army officers or expat bankers. We squeezed the Opel between twin Denalis and walked in through a gate in the town wall; I pushed Macy's empty stroller while Amy held her. At the platz a brass band played in the Christmas market and crowds swelled like tides beneath the high old buildings. We bought sausages and glühwein from a booth, then started the cycle through the tidy medieval streets. A couple of times Amy took pictures of me and Macy in front of a fountain or one of the leaning, half-timbered houses. I wasn't sure what to do with her—I'd only seen Macy a couple of times since that day in Langgasse—and I held her awkwardly against my chest or rested my palm on her head as she squirmed next to my leg. By the third picture I began to get nervous. I said something to Amy about it and she gave me a blank look and said, "I just want some pictures." I let it go.

"Jason would have loved this," Wesley said, stopped in front of a shop selling souvenir knives. Jason was Amy's ex-husband, from whom, she'd told me, she'd divorced a year ago. It was through him Amy and Beth had met, army wives at Fort Bragg. But Wesley's eyes were red. I looked to Amy and she was teary, too, and at that I felt the bottom of my stomach sink open. Amy caught me looking and said, "Please." I stayed quiet and we left soon after.

WHEN THE RED OPEL PULLED UP TO MY APARTMENT, Amy got out. She kissed the still-sleeping Macy on the forehead, then asked Beth, "You're sure you don't mind?" and Beth waved her toward me.

Once inside she told me what I'd already figured out, that Jason was dead, not divorced. He'd been killed a year ago in Afghanistan, she said. I started to say something, though I had no idea what, and she stopped me before I could.

"I needed to talk to you about all this tonight anyway. You get to stay ninety days without a visa."

"Okay," I said.

"My ninety days are about to run out."

I was a little stunned. "Really?" I said.

"I've got ten days—I have to leave a week from Monday. But if we got married—" She broke off, glanced away.

"I'm already married," I said.

"You could divorce."

"That would take time."

"Only thirty days in Michigan. I looked it up. I could go home, then come back once you were divorced."

I felt the blood drain from my body. The newly risen ghost of Amy's husband sat in the corner of the room. "My visa's only good until August," I said, to say something, even though she knew I'd been offered an extra year. Despite myself, I'd kept the university here happy. Unlike my predecessors, I had resisted throwing stacks of student essays in the toilet or claiming that people in the department were passing secret messages to me in their lectures.

"It's not just about staying here," she said. "I like you. I've been thinking about us, together."

She seemed her prettiest then, looking up at me. She shook with a slight tremor—she was fighting hard. And the truth was, I liked her, too. But as I stood over her, the twelve years that usually disappeared when we were together returned. All I could see was her watching her old reality TV shows dubbed in German, Macy throwing a fit, and me, who liked a silent apartment filled with nothing but the noise that drifted from the street, trying to read behind a shut door.

I told her she was being ridiculous, this wasn't what I'd wanted, and how could I trust her after today? For a moment her face remained still, but then she bolted up, hand jerked to hide her eyes, and rushed out. I stood there and watched her go.

NEARLY A MONTH LATER, the week after Christmas, I flew to London, summoned by Clara. Her sister lived in the Surrey suburbs, and Clara had flown over to visit. She asked me to come for a day, and there wasn't a way for me to say no. I took a late flight and spent the night in a bland, business travelers' hotel near Heathrow that Clara's sister's husband, still technically my brother-in-law, booked for me with his points.

In the morning I took a cab to Windsor Great Park, where I was to meet Clara beside Virginia Water. The cab driver dropped me off in a parking lot, and beyond the lot spread the park, or one corner of it. People were out, walking dogs they'd dressed in raincoats and plaid quilted capes. The trees were lifeless, their bare limbs seemingly all that kept the gray, pressing clouds from tumbling to earth.

Clara was up ahead, her back to me as she watched the swans floating in the lake. I called to her, and she turned. There was her auburn hair, spilling out of her parka's hood, there was her dainty pointed nose, red with cold. Seeing her, I felt the last months erased, as if I'd just come up from a dream.

"Do you want anything?" I asked, nodding at the concession cart a hundred yards away.

"Tea," she said.

I'd been nervous ever since Clara called to ask me over, and as I waited for the tea and my hot chocolate I studied the cart's case of British snacks and tried to think through what I might do next. I had a suspicion of what was happening, but still my mind refused to work.

After I gave Clara her tea we took the path that went to the right, up the eastern branch of the lake. For a while we said nothing and watched the trotting dogs. Then, as I was testing my hot chocolate—still scalding—Clara said, "Do you plan to move back in with me next summer?"

That had been the plan once, the idea that Germany would be a cure.

"I don't know," I said. "I've been trying not to think about it."

There was a pause. Then, with a changed, efficient tone I'd never heard from her before, she said, "Good. That's all I needed to hear."

I stopped, but she kept walking. I jogged to catch up with her. "What do you mean?"

"I'm going to file for divorce."

As we walked she kept a few inches between us. I sipped my hot chocolate. It was cooler now.

"Don't worry," she said. "I'll let you know what you need to do." In that moment I decided the last thing I wanted was to cause her more pain, so I told her I'd agree to whatever she asked.

We passed through a part of the path lined on both sides with chain-link fence. Behind the fence workmen had left tools and some kind of tractor.

"What have you been up to, anyway?" she said.

"Fucking a war widow," I answered. I tried to smile, like it was some kind of joke, and only when I kept walking did I notice that this time she'd stopped. I turned and saw she'd started to cry. I went to her, but she batted me away. Dog walkers passed us, shifting their eyes.

"Really?" she said. "That's what you're going to say?"

I tried to put my arm around her, but she backed from me. "You don't deserve anything," she said, and the words cut like broken glass.

I FLEW BACK TO FRANKFURT. On the plane I tried an exercise whereby I emptied my mind bit by bit. It didn't work.

From the airport I took the S-Bahn to Wiesbaden, and as we came to the Main I looked up, as I always do for rivers. I'd taken an early flight. The Main was still and narrow, and as the train turned to cross it the morning sun shot through the windows and the river suddenly glistened. Across from me two plump girls with spiked raven hair giggled over their cell phones, indifferent, their thick thighs stretching the weave of their matching leopard-print tights, their stout pimpled faces held close together. In the aisle a Turk or Romany, accordion folded shut and slung over his shoulder, shook his knitted change purse. I closed my eyes and listened as the bridge clacked beneath us. I felt Clara's words, Amy's silence, wounds beneath my skin. But the winter sun shone on my face and I said to myself: I am blameless. I said: I owe no one. I said: Surely something better has been promised me.

THE MOOR

The Moor's Origins

The earliest record we have of the black detective Jackson Hieronymus Burke—the Moor—is an advertisement he ran in several Berlin newspapers in 1873, promising discretion and modest fees. Nothing is known of his cases from this period, but, tracing the address given in the advertisement to one of the city's poorer quarters (Prenzlauer Berg), we believe they would have been limited to the lowest kind of work: finding stolen dogs, tracking suspected adulterers. After the advertisement, Burke drops from history until the fall of 1876, when he leaps onto the scene with a single feat of deduction.

All of Berlin had been baffled by the disappearance of the renowned theater critic Wolfgang Metzger. The police searched the sewers, dug up his mistresses' back gardens. They questioned actors whose abilities he had maligned, impresarios whose shows he had damned. Neither the body nor evidence of foul play was found. Then, two weeks later, a letter appeared in the newspaper: Metzger had not disappeared, but had murdered his twin, a wealthy hay merchant, and replaced him. The letter, signed by Burke, described how he had uncovered the truth when he visited the twin's villa to offer his services. He'd been directed to the stables and, finding the man there, noticed the horses shying from his touch. "With that I understood all," he added with the confident flourish he would keep for the rest of his career. The twin's servants might not have recognized a difference between Metzger and his brother, nor the twin's wife, but the horses, with their keen animal sense, had betrayed the critic, who had hoped, by impersonating his brother, to avoid his debtors.

The city was shocked by this revelation and amazed by its deliverer. Everyone had the same question on their lips: who was this man, and where had he come from? Even now we can only speculate. Burke never spoke of his past, nor of how he came to detection. One rumor holds that he was born a slave on a Texas sugar plantation in the early 1840s, another that he was the son of a New Orleans freedman. References in certain archives suggest that a black detective—called, simply, El Negrito—practiced in Havana during the Civil War, but no proof connects him to Burke. We only know that Burke was American, that he was in his thirties when he arrived in Berlin, and that at the start of his career—in which he would solve over seven hundred cases and be memorialized in dozens of dime novels—he already possessed powers to rival the French masters Vidocq and Devergie.

Soon Burke's photograph began appearing in shops, alongside etchings of the stable scene and a pamphlet, by a hack named Frisch, promising to teach its readers the detective's secrets. He was invited to dinners, asked to salons—it was now, in the flush of his first triumph, that a columnist for the *Zeitung*, remarking on Burke's color, gave him his nickname by declaring him their Othello, their Moor.

His Appearance

One must be wary of the newspaper and dime-novel illustrations, which often colored him darker than he was, thickened his lips, bulged his eyes. He was of middle height—five feet seven inches tall—and possessed a slight paunch, a rather large brow, and a strong nose with a rounded tip. His eyes were hazel, his skin a deep chestnut, his mouth often shaped into a slight smile that, as the kaiser famously remarked, simply said, "I know." He never cultivated a mustache, kept his hair cropped close.

As for his dress, he wore English-cut suits of either gray or black wool, his sole ornaments three watch fobs hung from a golden chain. The fobs never changed, and any schoolchild in Wilhelm I's Berlin could name them: the gold ship's wheel to commemorate the Rhine Barge Mystery, the miniature shield presented to him by the Munich police in honor of his role in solving the Dubbel Murders, and the platinum-mounted bear claw given to him by the Prince von Schlieffen after he rescued Christiana, the prince's intended, from her gypsy kidnappers. He wore them at all times—whether he was pursuing a clue in the sewers or lecturing the Reichstag on the criminal mind—perhaps as a warning of his constancy to those who would oppose him.

His Rooms, Part 1

Not long after the Case of the Murdered Twin—when he began receiving regular commissions and collecting handsome fees—Burke moved from Prenzlauer Berg to Fasanenstrasse, on the far side of the Tiergarten. He occupied the entire fourth floor of his building. Rooms upon rooms circled the courtyard, and over the years he fitted them out to his exacting specifications. There were the main living quarters, of course, and the famous sitting room where he met his clients while reclining on his settee—to heighten the flow of blood to his brain, it was said. Then there were the rooms for his collections: one for the ordered cartons of lint and hair from the chief criminals of the Continent and Britain; one filled with jars of soils from around the world, which he employed in the identification of dirts found at crime scenes; and one for weapons of every description: blackjacks and saps, trays of bullets and blades, a kris from the Dutch East Indies, even an atlatl from the polar regions. The chief of these rooms was the library. There he made his experiments, and there he kept his famous blue-morocco volumes—a vast collection of books and pamphlets, ranging from studies of African beetle carapaces to treatises on the patterns of broken glass, used in the study of clues.

His Mounting Fame

With each new case (the Mystery of the Blue Hussar, the Theft of the Archbishop of Mainz's Diamond Miter), his fame swiftly grew. German bakers began producing the Moor's Torte, a coffee-flavored pastry studded with "clues" (sultanas), and Moor Clubs spread across the Continent and in England—members blackened their faces and were given the details of a crime that must be solved by the end of the afternoon. Soon Burke was maintaining correspondence with other men of note (Kalb Ali Khan the philosopher-nawab of Rampur, Lord Roscomb the industrialist, Oscar Agardh the Swedish Darwin), and in 1884 he was summoned to Japan by Emperor Mutsuhito to solve the Golden Crane Murders plaguing the imperial family.

By 1881 one could open the newspaper on any given day, anywhere on the Continent and even in the United States, and read about Burke—that he had recovered a stolen painting for the State Museum or hunted the vitriol thrower Kurtz, that he had been seen having champagne with an actress at Dressel's or sitting in Prince von Ysenburg's box at the opera, or that he had received some new recognition from the kaiser or beaten the Prince of Wales at billiards. One famous article recorded the foods Burke ate in order to discover which aided his thinking (plums and kidneys, the reporter decided), while a number of others provided phrenological analyses of his skull, citing the enlarged organs of Comparison and Human Nature as the seat of his mental prowess.

His Nemesis

In the course of his career, Burke battled many adversaries: the confidence man Reynolds, the assassin Fiori, the archspy Countess von Perlitz. But greatest and most dangerous of all was the shadowy crime broker Heinrich Bloch.

In the fall of 1886, six-year-old Liesl von Eberbach, the daughter of the interior minister, was stolen from her home. Within a day letters began arriving at the papers bearing blood-spotted scraps of her dress. The letters asked no ransom, made no demands, but warned the girl would be killed in a week's time. None could understand the kidnappers' motive, nor find the faintest trace of their whereabouts—the letters bore postmarks from around the empire. Liesl's father called in Burke to investigate, and with only a water stain and a sample of dust he determined she was being held in the aquarium by two henchmen in the pay of Henri Guillard, the French ambassador's attaché. Liesl was rescued, the city relieved, the interior minister supremely grateful.

But Burke was not satisfied. He recognized in the plan's design a genius far beyond Guillard's. Its purpose, in terrorizing Liesl's father, was to force his resignation and cause the German government to fall. Burke couldn't question Guillard—he hid himself in the embassy, claiming immunity—but when he tried the henchmen they gave him a name, Bloch. They never met the man, they said, nor knew who he was. But it seems they had told Burke enough. The next morning they were found murdered in their cells.

In the months and years that followed, Burke devoted himself to the study of Bloch, yet he discovered little about the fiend, why he turned to crime or how he came to dominate it. The bastard son of Joachim Bloch, spice merchant, and his Javanese mistress, Heinrich Bloch was given the running of his father's spice house at a young age and used it as a front throughout his career. Living in the Nikolaiviertel as a simple burgher, Bloch kept a perfect cover. But Burke knew that Bloch arranged the bombing of Grand Duke Alexey's carriage during his state visit, masterminded the Reichsbank Jewel Robbery, and plotted the mine collapse at Augsburg, in which a hundred men died. It was said that Bloch controlled a network of a thousand criminals in the city; that he was a past master of the bassoon, his instrument having once belonged to the only man he'd killed with his own hands; that as soon as he'd planned and seen the execution of a thousand crimes he would retire from the spice house and return to Java and live on a boat; that he demanded souvenirs from each of his terrible schemes and kept them in pine cabinets: a golden bolt from Alexey's carriage, the preserved finger of one of the Reichsbank's murdered clerks, a lump of bloodstained ore from Augsburg.

For six years Burke pursued Bloch but failed to prove his guilt in any crime. Some claim that Burke could have done so, but that he took a connoisseur's pleasure in tracing each of Bloch's plots and allowed him his freedom to ensure there would be more. Most, though, find such a suggestion preposterous. At the end of six years, in the winter of 1892, Bloch disappeared. The spice house was boarded up. Every trace of Bloch was gone. When Burke mentioned this to the papers, he said he suspected some new villainy but could not name it.

His Rooms, Part 2

A tantalizingly brief mention in a catalog of homes of the celebrated, published in 1890 and discovered only recently, describes a room in Burke's house holding a dozen glass curios filled with ceramic blackamoors. "Some stand nobly, others ride steeds, and yet others kneel and bear gifts," the catalog reads. "Blackamoors of all shapes and sizes, bareheaded or in turbans and fezes." His clients sent them, which tells us much, but what tells us more is that he kept them. For all our research, Burke himself remains a mystery, yet here we have a clue. He had a passage of Pushkin engraved on a brass tablet and mounted beneath the central curio, which the catalog gives thus: "He felt that he was for them a kind of rare beast, a peculiar alien creature, accidentally brought into a world with which he had nothing in common." He was perhaps not as at home in Berlin as is commonly assumed, and with this passage as a lens we can see traces of a deep melancholy in Burke's dinners alone at the Café Bauer, his solitary trips to the shore.

There were yet other rooms whose contents we do not know,

entire hallways unrecorded by history. Here speculation enters. Perhaps he had a dozen bedchambers, choosing among them depending upon his temper. Sometimes, thinking of Burke's end, we picture him roaming the halls on a long night, never finding quite the right room.

His Love

Despite the invitations to hunting parties and long weekends at castles, or the occasional notice about his being seen with an actress, Burke's life was solitary. He explained this as a necessity of his profession, claiming in one of his more famous maxims that a detective must form few attachments. But that did not mean his heart was immune to tender feelings. Through careful study, we have discovered evidence of a great passion.

In the summer of 1885 Burke was called to Wiesbaden to investigate a spate of jewel thefts. While pretending to be on holiday—attending the spa's gatherings, circling the room with a glass of the waters—he met an Englishwoman named Olivia Ashdown. They were soon seen strolling through the Kurhaus Kolonnade and riding the funicular up the Neroberg, arms locked, engaged in long, close conversations. Never before had Burke so doted on a female. But the other bathers disapproved. Helmut Strauss, the noted horseman and one of Burke's acquaintances, warned him that he went too far, that all were talking of his dark hands on her white bosom.

Burke promptly broke with Olivia, but after he solved the case (an elderly waiter was the thief) he stayed in Wiesbaden for a week. Such lingering is unprecedented; he always returned swiftly to Berlin at a case's conclusion, yet this time he retired to a cottage above the city and sent for champagne and lobsters. Though the newspaper accounts make no mention of Olivia, it takes little effort to determine their break had merely been a ruse. When Burke finally returned to Berlin, the papers reported his surprisingly happy demeanor. With these details we have reconstructed the week he must have spent with Olivia: the long mornings in bed, the tender suppers in dishabille.

The evidence of Burke's relationship with Olivia is scant, but it weighs heavily. Three months after Wiesbaden he was dining at Dressel's when he received word of another rash of thefts, this time at Badenweiler. He left immediately, taking the express. Yet no record exists of the crimes at Badenweiler, nor at any of the other spa towns to which he was summoned every three months, and where he would stay for a week, lodged in seclusion outside town. He never commented on these "cases," except to call them delightful.

His Greatest Case

How does one compare Burke's cases, weigh the greatness of his reasoned deduction in one against that required for another?

The Wannsee Murder reportedly gave him the most fits. A body was found in an industrialist's hunting lodge, arranged on a bier of pages torn from directories and volumes of Goethe. No one could identify the dead man, who was stripped of all his clothes. Burke took months to solve the case. The oddest is the Ware Killing, in which the murderer hired Burke to solve both crimes. Or is it the Bamberg Mystery, in which the bludgeoned duke seemed to come back to life? Then there are the cases he solved in single sittings, like the Theft of the Frankenheim Clock, the Affair of the Red Letter, the Case of the Hidden Blackmail, and his recovery of Müller's collection of rare ferns, stolen in the light of day. Is that Burke at his most brilliant, his mind so keen he needn't leave his study? Such cases are too numerous to count. The case that caught the most international attention was that of the Taskmaster: an underclerk in a shipping office who had organized an army of women—the daughters of Duisburg's chief families—by sending them letters threatening them with slanders. He had ordered them to set fires for neither profit nor revenge, but for his pleasure alone.

When questioned on the subject, Burke would chuckle—a chuckle that stirred shivers in the listener, the reporters wrote— and say his greatest case was yet before him.

The Attempts on His Life

We know of three serious attempts made on Burke's life.

The first came one evening while he was leaving a theater. A man ran up to him and stabbed at him with a dagger. The attacker missed, the blade passing through Burke's coat, and was over- powered by a policeman. Burke identified him as Dr. Mildenberger, a government scientist who'd been ruined when the detective un- covered the Mosquito Ring's plot to steal the war ministry's supply of quinine.

Then the Black Lion, a band of anarchists that Burke had foiled multiple times, caught him halfway up the Siegessäule and shot at him. He escaped with only a slight wound.

In the third attempt, an assassin working for a consortium of villains—perhaps Bloch, though the connection was never firmly made—snuck into Burke's rooms with the intention of garroting him in his sleep. The assassin got lost in the halls, and as he wan- dered from room to room Burke crept up behind him and stuck him with a blow dart from his collection, putting him instantly to sleep.

Doubtless there were more, but they have not been recorded. Once, when asked about the attempts, Burke said he did not mind. "Let them come. Very well. But they mustn't touch—" At that he broke off. When pressed, he refused to say anything else, though it is generally agreed he was referring to the harrowing events of the Schott Affair, which had passed just months before.

The Schott Affair

Aside from the gossip at Wiesbaden, the only other specific mention of Olivia Ashdown in Burke's history—and perhaps the greatest evidence of his love for her—comes in the middle of his investigation of the murder of the mirror magnate Johannes Schott. In 1893 Schott invited his family, as well as Burke and several old army friends, to his country mansion to celebrate his birthday weekend. But just before the first night's dinner, Schott was found stilettoed in his study. At Burke's insistence the police sealed the mansion while he examined the rooms and conducted interviews, and by the next morning he had discovered Schott's son's gambling debts, his valet's true identity (he was Schott's nephew), and a suspicious ash pile in the garden. Burke was about to question the rest of the staff when he received an unsigned telegram. To the consternation of the police and the papers, Burke fled to Bad Kreuznach.

There, the telegram had told him, Olivia—later identified by the papers as "an unknown woman"—lay dying. She had been poisoned, and as the doctors treated her, Burke contributed his knowledge of antidotes. The toxin was rare, taken from the back of a Borneo toad, and, despite the telegram's warning, she had not been given a lethal dose. Once Olivia was beyond danger, Burke returned to the Schott mansion. Within an hour he identified the murderer as Schott's wife, and as he questioned her she confirmed his suspicions, confessing she had arranged Olivia's poisoning with the hope of stopping him. When Burke asked how she knew of his love, she answered, "I have a friend." Scarcely before the last word had passed from her lips, she fell back in her chair and a bottle of prussic acid, which she must have emptied when she heard Burke's steps outside her door, rolled from her hand.

The identity of Frau Schott's "friend" remains unknown. Some hold that it was Bloch, that he had stepped briefly out of retirement to give Frau Schott the plan, merely to unnerve Burke. Others believe Frau Schott was a secret devotee of the Reverend Stöcker, who, along with his attacks on Jews, had begun deriding the government's reliance on "this trained ape in man's clothes." At any rate, Burke's love for Olivia had become known to the criminal world, and now he had to choose between her and his profession. He endangered her, and she made him vulnerable: any fiend who wished to thwart him need only threaten Olivia. His decision seems clear. After the Schott Affair, the record of his cases contains no more false entries of jewel thefts in spa towns.

Des Mohren Dilemma

Not long after the Schott Affair, Burke received perhaps his highest honor. In the winter of 1894, an opera inspired by his career, Otto Hussner's *Des Mohren Dilemma,* opened in Berlin. Set in seventeenth-century Rome, *Des Mohren Dilemma* intertwines a detective, Burccino, with the fate of two unfortunate lovers, Alberto and Francesca. At first Burccino rebuffs their entreaties for help. By the opera's end he rushes to save them, only to find he is too late.

Two anecdotes survive from the opera's run. The first occurred during the second intermission on the opera's opening night, after Burccino has unknowingly aided the villain in his plot to divide the lovers. Burke was smoking in the salon, chatting with Prince von Ysenburg and a stoop-shouldered general, when a drunk Junker in a lancer's uniform accosted him. "You fool!" the Junker cried as he tottered up to him, taking hold of Burke's sleeve and scowling. "How could you? Those poor young things. How could you? Fool!"

All in the salon turned toward them, and for a moment Burke was startled. Then, he smiled and said, "I've been asking the same question. I find this Burccino rather blind." The strained moment passed—the Junker, swaying on his feet, was pulled away by his friends—and received only a slight notice in the papers. And yet is this incident not a brief foreshadowing of what was to come? The second anecdote concerns Burke's reaction to the opera itself, which he attended every night of its run. His constant presence became a piece of Berlin gossip; those in the audience noted that he always wept during Burccino's first aria, after Burccino refuses the lovers and laments that he was not fashioned for love but reason alone.

The Last Months

The next year, Burke worked with a frantic brilliance, crisscrossing the Continent, completing investigations in the span of hours, sometimes minutes. Stolen pearls in Nîmes followed by poisoned bread in Königsberg, blackmail in Prague followed by a kidnapping in Utrecht, counterfeiters in Worms followed by a druidic murder at Rügen. He turned nothing down, allowed himself no rest. For the first time since the Case of the Murdered Twin, he tracked lost dogs and followed adulterers. Observers noticed a sharp change in his behavior. He didn't smile. He was cruel to waiters, short with clients, dour with reporters. He ignored invitations to the Imperial Palace, and was cited twice for drunkenness, once for horsewhipping a prostitute. Except for the tinge of desperation that infused his labors, one might consider this period a florescence. It was as if he knew.

The Folsch Scandal

On December 5, 1895, the war minister visited Fasanenstrasse and disclosed to Burke a grave predicament. He had made a secret bargain with Russia: in exchange for three thousand Folsch rifles (whose precision was unmatched), the czar would quietly transfer a strip of land along the China Sea to German hands. But the rifles had been stolen in transit, and the czar's minister was furious, accusing the Germans of duplicity. Were the rifles not recovered, an international crisis would be unavoidable.

That evening Burke traveled to the far edge of Silesia, the site of the theft, and once there followed a set of subtle clues (specks of foreign soil in the snow, a dropped button, a twisted leaf) south and west across the Austrian frontier. At Pressburg he cabled the minister that he was certain the thieves were traveling by river barge. But the next day the minister received a disturbing report. He'd sent several of his own agents to aid Burke. They'd taken rooms for the night in a tavern, and when they called on Burke in the morning they found he was gone. His night candle was burned to a nub, unreadable notes and sketches lay scattered on his table, and his bed was unused, his small traveling bag still beside it, unpacked. There was no sign of a struggle, and the agents hoped Burke had simply taken a morning stroll to order his thoughts. But with each passing hour they knew: wherever he was and however he got there, he was already far away and would not be returning. The minister confined himself to his office and sent a barrage of conciliatory telegrams to the Russians while he awaited more news from his men, whom he'd ordered to search the riverbanks for Burke's corpse.

Then, three days later, Burke turned up in Istanbul. He was found by an Armenian dockworker in the hold of a barge. His mouth was gagged, he was tied to a chair, and the rifles were stacked behind him. On his lap lay a note: "To the Ottoman Government, with my Compliments—Bloch."

What happened next is at the same time baffling and inevitable. The papers accused Burke of treason—an accusation the minister encouraged, as it distracted from his own role in the blunder—and the people swiftly followed, hurtling rage at one who, not a week before, they had adored. Was it his color? Or that, so used to his successes, they could not understand his failure, could only interpret it as treachery? They said he had organized the theft of the rifles and planned all along to deliver them to the Turks. The *Berliner Kurier* claimed that for years Burke had been a secret agent of the Sublime Porte, that in exchange for the rifles he was promised a principality of his own and a fully stocked harem. They printed a cartoon of him dancing for the kaiser while in the background Sultan Abdul Hamid laughed. The *Münchner Telegraf* wrote that his brutish nature had finally overtaken him, that his being tied to a chair was a cheap ruse. The *Zeitung* interviewed Police Commandant Fuchs, who assured reporters there was no secret archfiend Bloch and excused Burke's claims otherwise as the delusions of an overstrained mind, while the *Frankfurter Abendblatt* opined that it was natural that the Moor should help the Ottomans. They referred to his duskiness, and to the blood of southern climes coursing through his veins.

When Burke returned to Berlin—the Turks kept the rifles but sent him back—angry crowds gathered beneath his windows in Fasanenstrasse, calling for his expulsion. He refused to defend himself, said nothing of how he'd been caught or what had occurred during the three days of his disappearance. Within a week he was confined, for his safety, to a cell in a police station near the Ostbahnhof, where he received news of each fresh development— that a mob had rushed into his apartment, overturning the shelves of soils; that the Moor Clubs had been swiftly disbanded; that, at the Reverend Stöcker's urging, people across the empire were building bonfires and burning the albums they'd filled with photographs and clippings of his adventures—with a stoic acceptance.

But by the time he was delivered to the French border, he was visibly broken: meek as an invalid, given to shaking. Our only record of him at this moment comes from the diary of a Sergeant Heinz. Not one of the newspapers sent a reporter, interest in the scandal having been swept aside by a suicide pact that had claimed a member of the general staff and a junior officer's wife. When Burke's guards let him go, he walked into the Belfort Gap and out of history. Some believe he settled in Tunis, others that he became a hotel detective in New York, but no one knows for sure.

The Final Mystery

Burke's life and career give rise to hundreds of unanswered questions, but, so many decades after, perhaps most vexing of all is the matter of those three days on the Danube. His complete silence on the subject has divided the followers of his career into two hostile camps. The first holds that everything is as it appears. Bloch trapped him. The villain's vanishing had been a ploy, giving him years to plot Burke's downfall. He planned every detail, foresaw every effect—even how signing his name on the note would only stoke the people's doubts. The proponents of this theory say it was only a matter of time, that even one of Burke's intellect must someday stumble. To pretend he couldn't, they claim, denies him the hallmark of humanity and puts any doubter in line with those who turned against him. He might have recovered from the scandal, they say, were he not a black man.

But others find this account laughable, call the appeal to humanity so much posturing, and counter that in ascribing such foresight to Bloch we rob Burke of any. They grant Bloch his scheme but argue that Burke would have been too clever to play into the fiend's hands. Noting his erratic behavior in the months leading up to the scandal, they suggest Burke wanted to retire. Knowing there would be constant demands for his return, that only if he were disgraced would he be left alone, he made perhaps the cleverest move of his career: he walked willingly into Bloch's trap, understanding all that would happen and seeing in it freedom.

There's no way of knowing what happened during those three days, how Burke came to be tied up in the barge's hold, and so we're forced to choose blindly between the two theories, the choice becoming less about the truth and more about the Burke the chooser prefers. But doesn't an opportunity lie in the absence of fact? That is why, taking elements of the second theory, we propose a third, one we've never shared: after Olivia's poisoning, forced to decide between her and his career, Burke chose as he should have—he chose love. At Olivia's bedside in Bad Kreuznach he plotted their retreat from the world, crafting the scandal—there was no Bloch on the barge, Burke arranged the theft of the rifles himself—not to aid the Turks but to ensure his fall. Only then would they be left alone to live out their years in peace and contentment, perhaps in the French countryside, perhaps on some Greek isle. There's no evidence, of course. The decision he made after Bad Kreuznach appears plain, as do its consequences. But as long as we don't know his end, why not grant him this last happiness? After all, where does history exist, except in our imagination? Does that make it any less true?

ACKNOWLEDGMENTS

The stories in this collection were originally published in the following:

"Byzantium" in *Electric Literature;* "East Texas Lumber" in *Harper's;* "The Don's Cinnamon" in the *Antioch Review* and *Best American Mystery Stories 2013;* "Borden's Meat Biscuit" in *Subtropics;* "The Traitor of Zion" in *Ecotone;* "Eraser" in *One Story* and *New Stories from the South 2010: The Year's Best;* "At Boquillas" in *The American Scholar;* "Tayopa" and "The Moor" in *Boston Review;* and "Amy" in the *Literary Review.*

Thanks to: The University of Michigan Hopwood Prizes, the University of Toledo's URAF Summer Research Award, the MacDowell Colony, the Corporation of Yaddo, Helen Herzog Zell, my MFA classmates and teachers, Jin Auh, Jacqueline Ko, Steve Woodward, and the Bread Loaf Writers' Conference.

BREAD LOAF AND THE BAKELESS PRIZES

The Katharine Bakeless Nason Literary Publication Prizes were established in 1995 to expand the Bread Loaf Writers' Conference's commitment to the support of emerging writers. Endowed by the LZ Francis Foundation, the prizes commemorate Middlebury College patron Katharine Bakeless Nason and launch the publication career of a poet, a fiction writer, and a creative nonfiction writer annually. Winning manuscripts are chosen in an open national competition by a distinguished judge in each genre. Winners are published by Graywolf Press.

2012 Judges

Tom Sleigh
Poetry

Randall Kenan
Fiction

BEN STROUD's stories have appeared in *Harper's, One Story, Electric Literature,* and *Boston Review,* among other magazines, and have been anthologized in *New Stories from the South 2010,* and *Best American Mystery Stories 2013.* A native of Texas, he now lives in Ohio and teaches creative writing at the University of Toledo.

The text of *Byzantium* is set in Minion Pro. Book design by Kim R. Doughty. Composition by BookMobile Design & Digital Publisher Services, Minneapolis, Minnesota. Manufactured by Versa Press on acid-free 30 percent postconsumer wastepaper.